MARY AND ME

TWO WOMEN WITH PARKINSON'S DISEASE
TWO HUNDRED YEARS APART

Robyn Cotton

Published by DayStar Books Ltd
PO Box 65275, Mairangi Bay, Auckland 0754, NZ

Copyright: Except for the purpose of fair reviewing no part of this publication may be reproduced or transmitted in any form or by any means, electronic or mechanical, including photocopying, recording or any information storage or retrieval system, without permission in writing from the author. Infringement is liable to prosecution.

© Robyn Cotton, 2021

ISBN: 978-0-9951356-5-9

Cover design: Betty McCready

Production by Outline Print Consultancy
Printed in New Zealand

Dedication

Mary and Me is dedicated to all those with Parkinson's disease: past, present and future. You are all heroes. I hope this story inspires you with hope, courage and positivity.

Acknowledgements

This project could not have been completed without the support and encouragement of my soulmate, Geoff. Living with Parkinson's disease is as much his journey as it is mine and he has helped me learn to live positively despite the disease.

I am indebted to Lesley, Alanah, Margaret, Robert, Sandie, Nancy, Mark, Janette and Glenys for their critical review and proofreading of my manuscript. A special thanks to the talented Betty and Al for their cover design. I am grateful to Parkinson's New Zealand for throwing their support behind this project, and to Daystar for agreeing to publish this book and for making the publishing journey easy.

A big thank you to those who contributed to my crowd funding, which has enabled me to get the book published in a way that allows the proceeds to be gifted to Parkinson's projects.

Finally, I want to acknowledge all my family, friends and health professionals who have inspired, guided, encouraged, humoured and stood with me as I've battled and come to terms with the alternate reality of living with Parkinson's disease. Without you in my life this book could not have been written.

Preface

My intention in writing this story is to raise awareness of Parkinson's disease, to give hope and to encourage everyone living with it to live positively and be as well as they can be. The messages in this book are especially relevant to those who are newly diagnosed and their families. While there are times when it can be difficult to see the positives, there is life after diagnosis and it can be a good life. The choices we make may impact how well we can live with this debilitating disease.

Many of the experiences included in this story are autobiographical. I acknowledge that I am fortunate to live a privileged life for which I am grateful. I also have a good support network of family and friends for whom I am also very thankful. My Parkinson's is mild compared to many sufferers and I was diagnosed at a time in my life when I was relatively young and fit. This has been to my advantage. I do not want to minimise the extent of suffering that others undergo, nor the difficulties that some people experience when trying to manage their symptoms, particularly when exercising.

From the time I was diagnosed with Parkinson's disease I embarked on a rollercoaster journey that took me from despair to hope. This is what I have attempted to capture in Mary and Me. I hope you will enjoy sharing this journey with me and that it will leave you encouraged and motivated to live positively with Parkinson's and to share this positivity with other sufferers.

Many of the characters in this story, their names and

some of the events, have been changed to protect the privacy of individuals.

I am not a medical expert and readers are urged to seek advice from their doctor before changing any Parkinson's treatments based on my story.

A glossary of terms has been included at the end of this book.

Robyn Cotton
April 2021

*What lies behind us, and what lies before us,
are tiny matters compared to what lies within us.*

Ralph Waldo Emerson

Mary and Me

1

James, London, 1810

She totters along bent forward over a stick, barely keeping her balance. Her eyes are downcast, not daring to look at the people who stare and shout insults. She is dressed in the rags of the poor; a tattered long grey dress under a soiled apron and a matted brown shawl around her shoulders. A basket over her free arm shakes as if it has a life of its own. A more wretched creature would be hard to find, but my curiosity is aroused, my compassion stirred.

We are in the Hoxton marketplace not far from my rooms, although I have not noticed this woman before on the streets of my neighbourhood.

She is moving through the market towards the bread stall when a group of youths appear from behind the barrels piled up beside the ale house. They are in the roughly-woven woollen breeches and shirts of the lower classes. Rounding the corner they spot the poor soul.

"Look at the old 'ag!" the smallest boy shouts, pointing a grubby finger at her.

"Git away, ye demonic 'ost!" A second boy jeers.

The largest of the boys, cap askew and looking menacing, picks a rotten apple out of a wooden box at the fruit stall and throws it at her. It hits her shoulder and splits, spurting juice across her face. She hastens her tortured gait.

"What's wrong? Too much of the spirits?" The boy's voice is full of cruel contempt. With a wicked grin, he selects an apple from a crate and takes a bite.

The greengrocer hurries out from behind his stall and shoos the boys away. I run to his side and the boys disappear before they are called to account for the apple.

Something compels me to follow her, perhaps out of compassion or perhaps medical curiosity. I want to talk to her, to understand her plight. I have observed similar symptoms before among some of my patients and it frustrates me that I do not know what causes this condition nor how to cure it. There is not even a definition for this malady and I am becoming increasingly convinced that it belongs to a new species of disease yet to be classified.

She shuffles along ahead of me with her head down as if trying not to draw attention to herself. Hostile stares are cast at her by vendors and customers alike. She purchases a small loaf and turns back towards me. As we draw close I can see her hair is unkempt and tangled, her pale face is lined and devoid of expression. But she is not ancient as her posture suggests—I guess she is in her early fifties.

I continue to follow her while studying her gait. Her propensity to lean forward forces her to walk on her toes and the front part of her feet. Her left leg appears weaker than her right, the foot barely lifting from the ground. Every five or six paces her left foot scuffs the uneven cobbles causing her to stumble. If it weren't for the crooked stick in her hand she might have fallen numerous times.

She enters a lane off the High Street that is flanked on both sides with housing institutions for the poor. I follow, keeping to the shadows. With a furtive look around, she enters an alms house through a low wooden door. These charitable institutions are known for providing rest to the poorest of outcasts, the most vulnerable, who without such charity would be starving on the street. It would be improper for me to knock on the door and I turn to walk out of the narrow street in the direction of my offices.

That evening I sit cogitating before my hearth, unable to find my usual comfort in a glass of fine French brandy and my favourite pipe. The image of the poor woman from the alms house is most perplexing. Her symptoms are not unlike those exhibited by three of my patients, albeit in different stages of decline. I believe it to be a pathology that is in the realm of science and not, as these sufferers believe, an evil from which they cannot escape. It is troubling that I cannot help them. What is most unusual about these cases is that their tremors occur when the afflicted limbs are at rest rather than when the muscles are at work. I have no choice but to make my observations and conjectures in the hope that they will offer a clue in the search for a cure.

*

Months later, I encounter the woman from the alms house for a second time. I remember her well and can identify her with certainty as the same woman. Once more our paths cross near the Hoxton marketplace.

She comes towards me, her face expressionless, staring down at her feet. A desperate sadness hangs over her and my curiosity is piqued. I must hear her story.

"May I speak with you?" I ask.

She ignores my request and her gait does not slow, although I swear her tremors increase in severity. Her tiny frame slumps even lower, as if afraid.

"Madam." My voice is louder this time. "Please may I speak with you a while? You need not be afraid. I am a physician and I would like to help you."

The face that looks up at me is small and oval with eyes that are wide and fearful like those of a child caught with its hand in the honey pot. I examine her face and am unprepared for the clarity and depth of blue in those unblinking eyes.

"Sir, what is it you want with me?"

"I would like to understand the condition afflicting you." I muster as much warmth in my voice as I can.

She looks away. "'Tis to me shame, sir." Her voice is feeble and without expression.

"It is clearly a malady. I have seen it before."

"Leave me be, sir. But be so kind as to give me some coin to buy me bread."

My fingers fumble inside my jacket and I find a shilling in my waistcoat pocket. Knowing this to be a fortune for this woman I pass it to her.

She reaches out and takes it from me with a trembling hand. "Thank you, kind sir." Her eyes seem to light up, but it is not reflected in her solemn face that remains a mask.

"May we sit in Hoxton Square and talk?" I ask.

She hesitates, perhaps unsure whether to trust me, then looks down at the shilling clenched between her fingers. Almost imperceptibly she nods, dropping the shilling into her basket.

We turn towards the Square where I guide her to a seat. Although the sun shines there is a cool wind that blows from the north and few people are about.

"Please tell, what is your name?" I ask.

"Mary Black."

"Please, would you be so kind as to share the story of your illness with me?"

"There is li'le to tell." Her speech is hesitant and her voice is weak and shallow, so low I strain to hear her words. "Some years back me left arm and leg began to shake. I 'ave li'le control over me limbs. Some say 'tis from alcohol consumption, but I ain't no alcoholic. Others say 'tis a demon who shakes me."

"Is it only on one side?"

"Yes, sir, me left side. It is as if me very limbs will not follow me will, like I am the puppet of a cruel and evil puppeteer."

"Madam, please continue. What else ails you?"

She hangs her head. "People avoid me."

"Please tell."

"Once I could write in a ledger, but now I ain't able to accomplish it." She looks away as she continues, her voice trailing off, "Me 'usband owns a small sweet shop and once I kept the ledger for 'im."

"Where is your husband now?"

A long silence ensues and I am afraid she is done with talking. But then she says in a voice barely more than a whisper, "'e threw me out onto the street. 'e was too ashamed of me. Said I were affectin' 'is business."

My heart goes out to this poor wretched soul and I ask softly, "What do you mean you were affecting his business?"

Tears form in her eyes and flow down her cheeks, streaking the dirt in their wake. She wipes them away with the back of her hand. "Li'le nippers were afraid of me, their mothers said I was demon possessed. It was bad for business."

"Madam, I am so sorry," I offer. "Is this why you are now in the alms house?"

She looks at me sharply. "Sir, 'ow do you know where I reside?"

It is my turn to feel shame. To tell her I had followed her would be unthinkable. "I have seen you before."

She looks down at the trembling hand in her lap. "Yes, they 'ave taken me in. But I fear not for long. It is a religious establishment and Mrs Oldham, the owner, says if I cannot be delivered of the demon I must leave. She does not want it to infect others. She says I ought to seek refuge in the St Luke's Mental Asylum."

"I do not believe this to be a form of demonic possession. Indeed, the demon is merely your own nervous system. I believe you suffer from a slow and debilitating disorder that affects your movement. This disorder is not well understood."

I stroke my beard in thoughtful attitude. I have heard similar stories before. The harsh reality they face is a society that not only discriminates against them but one that prefers superstition to science. To deliver these poor wretches would mean their condition must be known as a medical one and not the result of demonic possession.

"How else do you suffer?" I ask.

She answers slowly in her halting speech. "Sir, I ain't able to eat respectably. Me broth slops from the spoon and me fork frequently fails to raise a morsel from the plate to me mouth, or I raise it only to drop it or miss me own mouth entirely. 'Tis as if the puppeteer 'as control over me fork. The same for me drinkin' cup. Mrs Oldham forbids me making a mess and instructs other women to feed me." She pauses, before adding, "Some of the women shove the spoon at me and laugh when food runs down me chin."

I find myself fascinated by her condition and more so for her openness. "Madam, can you stop the shaking?"

She lifts her left arm and, perhaps through strength of will, the wearisome agitation stops. I pull out my fob watch—five, ten, fifteen seconds. Her hand begins to shake involuntarily with increasing intensity.

I am curious and need to know more. It is improper to touch a woman stranger but I must know. "Please, will you humour me a moment and try to push my hands away?" I hold up my hands.

She looks at me strangely, then slowly lifts her hands and reaches out to push mine.

"Harder." I push back ever so gently.

"Sir, 'tis me very best."

I detect a difference in the strength of her arms behind her push. She drops her hands to her lap and the tiresome trembling returns.

"I wonder if you would be so kind to please tell me more of your story to help me understand how this condition has progressed from when it first started."

"Forgive me, sir, for I am unaccustomed to conversation."

With that, she begins to tell her sad tale in striking detail. I am enchanted and lean in close so as not to miss a word. The more she tells the more animated she becomes.

Eventually she concludes and her big blue eyes hold my gaze, imploring me.

"Sir, can you 'elp me? Can you cure me? I would do anything. I ain't got much, but I wish to end this sufferin'."

"Madam, I wish I could but alas I cannot. We do not know what causes this condition or how to rid you of it."

She looks down. New tears escape, glistening in the sunlight like fine jewels. She takes a grubby cloth from her apron to wipe her face. "I am so ashamed. I try to 'ide, away from the cruel jests of the other residents. Please sir, do not misunderstand. A few of the women are kind souls and take time to 'elp me. But many are 'eartless. And when I step outdoors even strangers 'url insults and sometimes more. Pray tell me, what is it that I 'ave done wrong? 'Ow is it that I 'ave transgressed?"

"No, you must not think this way. I believe it to be a sickness not of your making."

She picks up her basket and rises slowly to her feet. The crooked stick wobbles under her weight. Those unblinking eyes stare through her mask as if she has seen an apparition.

"Thank you, sir."

For what, I wonder.

I stand and tip my hat. "I bid you farewell, Mrs Black."

But she has already turned away and is making her tortured walk back the way we have come. I watch her go, troubled that I cannot ease this woman's plight.

Once a privileged woman who had been given the opportunity of learning to read and write. And once the wife of a respectable shopkeeper. Now a victim to an unknown malaise and subject to the torments of an ignorant society. How many more Mary Blacks are hiding away? It is unlikely she and the poor souls like her will seek medical help. But even if they did, what can be done? The suffering, without the recognition of a disease, must be substantial; not only physical, but also mental and emotional.

I am left with an immense feeling of helplessness that is all encompassing. I have no tonic, I know of no operation, no intervention to put an end to this wretched malady. There is no label that I can attach to it. I am not even sure it is a single ailment, but there is a pattern I have observed in those who have similar symptoms. I am becoming increasingly convinced it is a type of palsy, *paralysis agitans*.

I waste no more time and hurry home to write up my notes.

My name is James Parkinson, Medical Practitioner.

2

Rose, Auckland, January 2017

I never realised two words could mean so much. Hold so much fear, so much dread. More than a threat—a life sentence. Just two words. Five syllables. That's all. *Parkinson's disease.*

I expected to come out of this appointment with a plausible explanation for my shaky arm, something with a cure.

For years there have been occasions when my hand has shaken uncontrollably, causing me to spill drinks. But these were intermittent and so I hadn't bothered to follow it up. Nearly thirty years ago my first rib was removed after issues with the nerve in the thoracic cavity. I assumed these recent problems related to that nerve damage, never thinking for a minute that it could be a neurological disease. One time, as far back as the late nineties, a colleague and I were on our way to a meeting when I experienced a bad tremor. It caused me to spill my coffee all over the floor. The time it took to clean up the mess made me late for an important meeting and my embarrassment turned it into a lasting memory.

It was two years ago that my tremor became more persistent. My doctor sent me to a neurologist who said it was an essential tremor and therefore benign. He said it definitely was not Parkinson's, based on his observation that my tremor was on both sides. Within minutes of being in his office he'd asked me to draw a spiral starting with my right hand. I was nervous and, being a leftie, I held the pen awkwardly. The resulting spiral had a few bumps. He said it was obvious from the spirals I drew that I had a tremor on both sides, but I was doubtful as I hadn't felt any tremor on my right side. I repeated the spiral test when I got home and, although still awkward, my right hand drew a spiral without any bumps, leaving me to question his diagnosis.

Eventually I went back to my doctor to ask for a second opinion—still hoping for the diagnosis I wanted, one with a cure. Perhaps some form of neurosurgery would be offered to correct the problem. When it moved into my left leg I should have known. When my GP felt my triceps and remarked there was some ratcheting in the muscle instead of smooth movement, again I should have known. Deep down, perhaps on some subconscious level, I buried my fear.

Parkinson's has no cure, just a downhill slide to a pitiful end. And I know what the end can look like. I visited my auntie each week as she lay in her rest home bed, weak and unable to communicate or move. I try to shut out the image of her suffering, but I hear my mother's voice, *You are so like your Auntie Margaret!* It's true that I do resemble her in physical ways as well as sharing some of her mannerisms. Now to share the same disease, the same sad destiny, is not something I'm willing to entertain.

Sitting in the neurologist's carpark, eyes streaming, I try to make sense of it. I feel alone. Now what?

My tremor is shaking up a storm—an unwelcome reminder. Stress always makes it worse.

I drive, barely able to see the streets. Where? I don't know, just away to somewhere, anywhere, a place I can cry without being recognised. I find myself heading towards Westhaven Marina and pull into the carpark. My face is wet, tears drip from my cheeks. I barely notice the odd stares from people who pass by.

My phone chirps. I know who it is. I don't trust myself to talk yet I answer it anyway.

"Hi."

"Hey babe, how was the appointment?" His voice has the familiar warm tone.

"Yeah, good." It's all I can manage.

"What did he say?"

A deep breath and I muster all my strength to sound in control. "I'll tell you after work."

"What did he say? Tell me now." This time more forcefully.

I can't lie to him. "He thinks it is early-onset Parkinson's disease." There—it is out. I said it and now I must own it.

"I'm on my way, where are you?"

"It's okay, you stay at work and I'll see you later."

"No, I'm coming now." I can hear the sob in his voice as the reality begins to sink in. "We'll face this together," he adds, his voice quieter.

I tell him where to find me and I just sit. Staring, not seeing. Processing. Numb.

Gary arrives. Goodness knows how he got here so quickly. He's been working in Auckland for the last two days and I drove up this morning just for my appointment. His car barely comes to a stop when he flings open his door and races around to me. As I get out, he pulls me to him, crushing me in a desperate embrace. His tears are wet on my shoulder. Tremors radiate from my left leg onto his steady body.

We find a quiet corner in a café and order some lunch.

"Now tell me everything." His voice is so full of concern. His beautiful eyes are moist and slightly puffy.

I relate it all. How the neurologist watched as I walked down the hall outside his office, being pulled gently backwards by the shoulders, repeatedly touching my index finger to my thumb, having to tap my feet in quick succession, and so on. I tell him the diagnosis is based not only on the tremor, but also on my muscles having a ratcheting type movement as well as slowed movements or bradykinesia. The neurologist said Parkinson's disease is unique to each individual, that there is no cure. Drugs and exercise will help with the symptoms. These are easy to relate—facts not feelings. When I tell Gary about the drug choices it dawns on me that I will be reliant on drugs for the rest of my life. This sounds like a punishment to someone who resists taking even paracetamol. I tear up again and let them run down the salty trails on my cheeks.

Gary reaches across the table to take my hand in his. In a moment I regain control, but when I look up at him tears are flowing freely down his cheeks.

"I asked the neurologist about the drug side effects and he told me not to focus on them, that not everyone gets side effects and they get blown out of proportion. How-

Mary and Me

ever, he did say if I have a penchant for something it may become an obsession. Like, if I like to shop for shoes—I could find I have a wardrobe full of them. Or alcohol and drugs—I could become addicted to fine wines."

"Not likely."

I chuckle. "Maybe I'll become even more addicted to sailing and cross over from a fair-weather sailor to an all-weather sailor."

Although we're a sailing family I prefer sailing in good weather and tend to put the handbrake on more adventurous voyages. The little bit of humour in this statement doesn't get lost on Gary and it helps release some of the tension.

"Or more hooked on me," he adds quickly, with a wry smile.

"I think I could cope with that." My smile is genuine, the first since those two little words were spoken over me.

"What exactly is Parkinson's disease?" Gary asks.

"I don't really understand it and I'm not sure I've remembered all he told me. But there's a part of the brain that controls movement and produces the dopamine that's needed for the body to function. The neurons that produce the dopamine die off. Apparently up to seventy per cent have already died by the time of diagnosis and you can't get them back."

"There's your first challenge. You need to do some serious research so you understand what we're dealing with."

I love his use of *we* and am in no doubt that he means we're in this together.

"What else did he say?"

"He asked me things that I wouldn't have thought were related, things that I've simply brushed off as not important. It seems that Parkinson's disease is a lot more than a tremor."

"For instance?"

"Well, there's my handwriting. Do you recall how I've complained my writing is becoming more difficult to read? It's been getting smaller, with the loops now barely visible. The doc asked if my handwriting had changed and said it was typical in Parkinson's patients."

"That's truly bizarre."

"Sure is. I can't fathom why it could possibly be an issue. It's truly weird how even when I try to make it legible my hand defies me and I don't seem to be able to form nice round loops."

"What else is related?"

"He said my arm doesn't swing when I walk and that it's another early symptom of Parkinson's."

Gary looks pensive. "I had thought that might be a family trait since you walk a bit like your dad."

"But Dad doesn't have a tremor or any other Parkinson's symptoms. The neurologist said the disease is thought to start in either the gut or the olfactory gland. Often patients lose their sense of smell early on but thankfully I still have mine."

"You are such a super-nose. I'd even go so far as to wager you have a keener sense of smell than normal."

"Thanks." I momentarily screw up my nose. "I guess that means you'll have to keep me in expensive perfumes.

I'll still be able to recognise the cheap ones that smell like air freshener."

He grins. "They're meant to be more for my benefit than yours."

I pause for a moment before getting serious again. "It seems likely that my history of poor gut health is linked to it—could even have been my first symptom."

My gut health has never been great. As early as my twenties I have been prodded and probed and labelled with irritable bowel syndrome.

"That's interesting. What else?"

"Do you recall my complaining years ago, perhaps in my thirties, of being really stiff first thing in the morning? I assumed it was just the ageing process and everyone must feel it."

"Vaguely."

"Rigidity goes with Parkinson's so that could also be related to it. I asked him about dementia, 'cos you know how bad I am at remembering names and numbers." My friends and I always joke about this, claiming it to be post-menopausal. But is it? Or is it Parkinson's?

"You don't have a problem any more than anyone else our age."

"Yeah, he said it's unlikely as only a small percentage get dementia and it's generally late in the process."

His face blurs in front of me as my tears overflow. I quickly wipe them away with the back of my hand. I focus on a distant spot, forcing my tears to stop.

"Did the neurologist give any advice about what to expect going forward?"

"Not really. He did say that exercise is important and, if I do nothing else, I should make that a priority in my day. He said stress can make it worse."

"Then we need to think about minimising your stress and making time for exercise."

"He also said I should contact Parkinson's New Zealand and get in touch with their local community nurse educator. She'll be able to point me in the right direction for support." I pause, holding his gaze for a long moment as I consider the enormity of my life sentence. I dab my wet cheeks with the napkin. "I am so very sorry. This is not what I wanted for us."

"Hey, it's okay. We're in this together and we'll work our way through it. In sickness and in health—right?"

I nod.

"Look, I'm really sorry I wasn't at the appointment." His gaze briefly holds mine before looking away.

"It's okay. Neither of us expected this outcome. You're here now."

"I'm going to take a few days off work."

"That's not necessary. I'll be okay."

"I need the time to get my head around it. You know how I process things. I take more time than you."

"There's no point moping about. You're probably better off at work. Besides, I have a client meeting tomorrow and I can't cancel."

The waitress puts down a plate of steaming quiche in front of me and I give a cursory thank you. I automatically pick up my knife and fork but put them back down, no longer tempted by the quiche. Gary eagerly tackles his burger while I play with the utensils, turning them around and around on the table. My left hand begins to shake uncontrollably, knocking the fork against the crockery plate. I put it back down and sigh loudly, hating my tremor.

He looks up. "Not eating?"

"No, I feel a bit queasy."

"You should try and eat something."

"I can't. Maybe later."

My pulse races, creating a light fluttering in my chest. Goosebumps prick my skin as a chill sends an involuntary shudder through my body, as if my blood was running cold.

We sit in silence, lost in our own thoughts. It's like I'm an actor in someone else's life. This can't be happening to me. How can I, a 56-year-old woman, carry the life sentence of a degenerative disease? Was he mistaken? Should I seek another opinion? Parkinson's is for the elderly, like Auntie Margaret. And yet something tells me it all adds up.

"Are you okay?" Gary frowns.

"Yes, no, I don't know." I add, whispering, "I'm scared."

"Don't be. We'll be okay."

"I'm too young to get an old person's disease." I look down at my fingers fidgeting with the napkin. "And it's just not fair on you to have to live your healthy retirement with a wife who's a burden. We won't be able to do half of what we've planned."

"You could never be a burden to me. Don't ever think that. We'll deal with this together. We might have to change our plans a bit, but we can do it. You're strong."

I stare out at the boats without really seeing them, not at all convinced we can deal with it. This is bigger than us. Bigger than anything we've faced in our marriage. This is something we cannot fix. We're in our mid-fifties, a time when we've done the hard yards and we should be planning our next adventures. It is so unfair.

Poor Auntie Margaret. Towards the end her thin, pale body was scarcely more than translucent skin on bones. Rigid limbs and the inability to communicate had turned her body into her prison. Her eyes stared out through an expressionless face, silently pleading, able only to hint at the agony of a life stolen by this ugly disease. How I disliked the pitiful sounds and the unpleasant smell of the rest home. Poor Uncle David would sit at her side for hours, receiving little or no response. Will this be our future? The vision is too much. I look away, trying to shut the memories out. Before they were hard, now they are terrifying. I try to console myself. I am not my Auntie Margaret. The specialist said each patient with Parkinson's is unique with their own set of symptoms and reactions to the drugs. I am me.

I may be strong, but I'm scared.

We ask for my lunch to be put in a doggie bag and Gary settles the account. As we walk to our cars he takes my hand firmly in his. It's reassuring to know that he'll always be there to support me no matter how tough things get.

We drive home in convoy. Normally I enjoy the trip—over the Bombay Hills, through the rolling farmland of the Waikato before ascending the Kaimai Range and coming down into the Bay of Plenty that is home. But today is different. Today I just want to get home.

The hands-free kit for the phone chirps. It's Gary.

"Hi, just wondering how you're doing," he says. "And wondering what you'd like for dinner."

"I haven't even thought about dinner."

"You don't need to. I'll cook," he says. "Are you okay?"

"I'm fine, just trying to process. You'll be pleased to know I've eaten the quiche."

"Good, you need to look after yourself, especially now."

I talk in a monologue; it helps me process. Gary makes only the occasional response and I know he's not ready to talk. I imagine he would prefer to take the news and put it in a sealed box that he can file away in a deep dark place, and only when it can't be avoided any more will he take it out to face it.

"I'm so very sorry," I say.

"I don't want to hear you apologise. There's absolutely nothing to apologise for. Stuff happens and we'll deal with it as best we can."

"But it's so unfair on you."

"Hey, let's not have any more of this talk. It won't help. I'm here in sickness and in health, remember?"

"We need to tell the kids."

"We can do that when we get home. Just focus on getting there safely."

"Okay, talk soon."

We hang up. In need of a distraction I turn on the radio. My brain defaults to autopilot, my mindlessness providing a much-needed refuge. Barely aware of my surroundings, the rest of the kilometres seem to pass faster now.

Once home Gary pours me a large glass of red and insists I retire to the lounge while he cooks dinner.

I sit in stunned silence, slowly sipping my wine. Too scared to think. I barely notice the room dim as shadows gather outside. Moving lights dance in the darkness from the television going in the corner, but I choose to ignore it. The words are just noise. I don't care about the news. I don't want to hear about the rest of the world. I have Parkinson's.

The lights come on as Gary walks into the room. "Dinner will be ready soon."

I force a smile. "Okay, thanks."

"We need to tell the kids," Gary says. "Are you up to making the calls while I finish in the kitchen?"

"Sure, I'll message Lauren and set up a time to WeChat."

"You should ask her to have Paul with her as she'll need him. It will be hard hearing this news in China and not being able to be here with us while we work it out."

"I'll message her and find out when they're available. They should be finishing at the school anytime now."

Our daughter Lauren, and her husband Paul, have been teaching in China for the last four and a half years. I miss her terribly and can't wait to have them home once their contracts end.

I message Lauren and, while I wait for her response, I punch in the number for our son. Michael picks up on the second ringtone.

"Hey Mum, how was your appointment?"

There's never an easy way to tell bad news. It just needs to be said.

"That's what I'm calling you about." I pause to take in a deep breath. "I've had some not so good news."

A pregnant pause, before Michael asks, "What is it?"

"He thinks I have Parkinson's disease." I say it softly, as if by not giving it volume it will reduce the life sentence.

Another pause, this time longer. "Like Auntie Margaret?"

"Yes, but I have my own version of it."

More silence.

"Mum, I'm so sorry. How're you feeling?"

"Gutted, but we'll cope. Just trying to get my head around it."

"That sucks."

"Tell me about it." Then realising I must be strong for our family, I add, "Look it's not so bad, really." I try to sound convincing. "It could be worse, a whole lot worse. It could be an imminent death sentence, but it's not."

Gary joins me as Michael bombards me with questions. I try to answer with all that I've learned in the last eight hours and all that I remember of my auntie's illness.

After a short while I hang up. Lauren has messaged to say she and Paul are free, waiting for my call. With a deep breath I make the connection and their faces fill my little screen.

"Hi Mum, what's up?" Lauren asks.

Again, I figure it's best just to say it as it is. "I've had my appointment with the neurologist and he says I have early-onset Parkinson's disease."

"I thought it was an essential tremor and nothing to worry about." She frowns.

"I went to a different neurologist in Auckland today for a second opinion."

Paul moves to put his arm around her, as tears slip soundlessly down her cheeks.

"Like Auntie Margaret." She says it as a statement and not a question.

"Yes, however the doc says every case is different and so we shouldn't compare."

Silence follows, as they absorb the news.

"Don't worry, I'll be fine. I have a prescription for drugs and the neurologist says I need to keep exercising." I fight to sound braver than I feel.

"Mum, I don't know what to say."

More silence. I desperately want to hug her. China is so far away and not for the first time I wish matter-transfer had been invented.

I fill the silence by talking about what the specialist said and I reassure them that I'm up for the fight. Our beautiful, strong daughter appears shell shocked. I recall the feelings of devastation and helplessness when Gary's mum got sick and we were living on the other side of the planet. It's so hard to be distant from family when things go wrong.

"I wish I was there with you." She wipes her face with the back of her hand.

"Me too. But it's only six months until your contracts finish and the time will fly by. We can't wait to see you both."

We finish the call and I turn to Gary. "That was hard. I feel exhausted."

"You did well. What do you think of their reaction?"

"They were upset, as you'd expect. What did you think?"

"I think Michael took it in his stride and Lauren reacted in a similar way to me—stunned and not yet ready to talk about it."

"It made me realise I need to dig deep, for all of us."

"You will, I have no doubt on that score. I would have struggled to have the conversation with the kids tonight. It's still too raw for me."

"I feel like I don't have an option. I need to own it while at the same time I don't want it to define me. I have to believe I can fight and stay me, not become that *Parkinson's patient*."

His face is full of anguish. "C'mon let's have some dinner."

I follow him to the kitchen, where he takes plates of steaming food out of the oven and carries them to the table before going back for the open bottle of red. "Here, I think tonight you could do with a second glass."

I hold out my glass for him to top it up. "We need to think about how it's going to affect our future."

"Look, I'm nowhere near ready for that conversation. There's no urgency, so let's leave it for a bit. I don't imagine things will change, not for a long time."

"But we need to talk about our future. What will happen to us now?" I persist. "How will it change things? I need to understand the implications, for us."

"Tonight, give yourself a break and let's just chill. It'll take time for it to fully sink in—I admit it's going to take me quite some time to come to terms with it."

I recognise a familiar tension. Gary tends to internalise his feelings and I process things verbally. We've been here before. I let it drop and try to hide my hurt.

We eat our dinner, exhausted with all that has happened, and opt for an early night.

3

Rose, Tauranga, January 2017

In one day everything has changed. Yesterday I met with the neurologist and today I am different. Older. Sick. And yet, in one day, nothing has changed. The sun rose in the east just as it did yesterday and everything looks as it did before my diagnosis. My symptoms are the same today as they were the day before yesterday when I was happily ignorant of what is going on inside my body.

But now I wear a label. I have Parkinson's disease, and my hand and leg shake as if broadcasting this fact to the world. This is me, a Parkinson's patient.

I go through the motions of preparing my espresso, a task I normally enjoy, but this morning it's more of a chore. Once brewed, I pour the delicious nectar into my favourite mug with the milk warmed to just the right temperature. With it in my left hand and the muesli bowl in my right, the mug wobbles uncontrollably and the precious liquid slops over the bench. Silently I curse, hating my tremor. I mop up the spillage and carry the bowl to the table before making a return trip for the coffee. *This is nothing. Wait until you can no longer feed yourself.* A lone tear escapes and makes its way down my cheek.

Why me? Why now? I'm not even old enough to retire. How long have I got before I can't work or function normally? Am I to become a burden on others? Will I end up as a burden for Gary? How can I now tap into my full potential and achieve my goals? So many questions, so many unknowns.

I call my friend Evelyn to share the news. I know she'll understand because her mum had Parkinson's and right now I could do with a friend.

"I saw a second neurologist yesterday and guess what he said?" I don't wait for an answer. "He thinks I have early-onset Parkinson's disease."

Silence.

"Rose, I'm so sorry."

"Not half as sorry as I am."

"Were you expecting that diagnosis?"

"Sort of, but it still came as a shock."

"You know my mum had it. She went down to the gym every morning at the retirement village and exercised for an hour. I think she may have had it relatively mildly. It never really got that bad for her."

Evelyn's mum had been a smart, stylish lady and I remember being surprised at how well she always looked.

"The neurologist said I need to make exercise the most important thing in my day."

"Don't take this the wrong way, but if there was one of our friends that had to have Parkinson's disease I would pick you."

This wasn't what I was expecting to hear and for a moment I am floored as the weight of her words hit me.

She continues, "You are probably one of the strongest people I know and if anyone can deal with it you can."

Unsure what to make of this I change the subject and navigate my way to safer ground. We talk about my upcoming book launch for my debut novel, which I've based on a personal trauma endured when I was 21 years old. It tells the story through the eyes of a young woman modelled on my character and experiences as well as the parallel story of the offender through his eyes.

A few more exchanges and we hang up. I sit and look at the phone, drinking coffee and mulling over her words. I'm a good candidate for Parkinson's disease because I am strong. It is true, I am a fighter. I've proven it in the past and I can prove it again, except this time I have no control over the problem, no control over the outcome. It isn't a mind over matter issue. The doc said it's already taken up to seventy per cent of my dopamine-producing brain cells and I can't get them back. Strong or not, what I need is a miracle.

Remembering my business meeting I check the time to find I'm running late. I race to get ready and, as always happens when rushing, my tremor becomes a continuous rippling movement down my entire left side.

I select a favourite top and pair of trousers then begin to get ready. When I've only one leg in my pants I nearly fall backwards but steady myself just in time. My balance has been noticeably deteriorating, presumably yet another Parkinson's symptom. I try again. Then with my arms lifted through the armholes of the top, a sharp pain grabs at my left shoulder like the tearing of a muscle. I wince and double over to ease it on. Somehow this makes it bearable. A quick check in the mirror reveals a rogue mark. In my hurry to change my top I lift my arms up to slide it over my head. The pain is intense. Tears flow and I'm defeated. This is my future. I bend over with my elbows down and ease it over my head before taking it down my arms and letting it fall in a pile on the floor. I replace it with a button-through blouse.

Poised with the mascara wand in my dominant left hand I study my enlarged reflection in the makeup mirror and will the tiny tremors to stop. I seize the moment and dab the brush at my lashes. Black smudges appear above and below and I curse as I look for a cotton bud to remove the mess. My irritation makes my tremor worse and my eyes well up with tears. I will not give in. I breathe deeply and try to relax. This time I brush it onto the lashes and, although not perfect, it's good enough. I gather my things and leave the house.

An hour later I pull into a visitor's carpark outside my client's office. My hand dances around to some secret melody. Thinking how good I could be in a dance group causes a brief smile, releasing some of the tension. It's a short walk across the carpark to the reception but just long enough to suppress my fears and doubts—new emotions where once I basked in self-confidence. I straighten my shoulders, lift my head and stand tall. I will not give in to this thing that seems intent on stealing not only my dopamine-producing brain cells but also my self-esteem. *I can do this.*

After a short wait I'm taken into the meeting room. Bright-eyed men and women sit around a central table, filling the small room and I feel the pressure to meet their expectations. As if on cue my hand tremor increases dramatically. It's become a sign for nervousness or stress. It

Mary and Me

seems the more stress, the more tremor, which makes me anxious and the tremor worsens. How I've changed. Once I was confident and self-assured and would've thrived in this moment. When had the adrenaline rush that came with a little positive stress been replaced by a tremor and a lack of confidence? What comes first, stress or tremor—a chicken and egg scenario. I try to ignore my shaking.

We begin the meeting with introductions before I outline the agenda. I pick up a whiteboard marker pen and it performs a dance of its own. All eyes are on it as if mesmerised, their faces openly conveying curiosity. Resentment towards my tremor flashes, distracting me from the task at hand. My audience is transfixed. Are they even hearing my words? Does my tremor make me less credible? Might they assume I also have early-stage dementia?

"Look, there's something I need to address. I have a tremor and it's been diagnosed as early-onset Parkinson's disease. If it doesn't bother you it won't bother me." There, I said it.

All eyes lift from my hand to my face. Relieved, I continue with the meeting.

I move to the whiteboard and begin to draw a diagram to demonstrate a point. The lines are bumpy and the words messy. It looks more like a child's drawing rather than that of a professional.

"I'm really sorry for my poor handwriting. It's a struggle to write neatly with a tremor." My audience looks unfazed and I realise the issue is mine, not theirs.

I soon find myself in the old and familiar zone, absorbed in discussion and leading the group towards the desired outcomes. Progress is good. Once again I move to the whiteboard with a pen, this time to capture the key points. Weirdly, no matter how hard I try to make nice round letters they come out small with barely any loops. And the words that follow each bullet point track strangely upwards and not in the straight line I intended. The faster I try to write, the worse they become. It's as if my hand is not connecting with my brain.

"Would you like me to do the notations for you?" Linda asks.

Embarrassed, I accept her offer and pass her the pen. I will need to get better at accepting help.

The rest of the meeting runs according to plan. I leave knowing I performed well and that my client is satisfied with our progress. More importantly my confidence is restored, at least for now, and I know I haven't entirely lost it. The gap between perception and reality can be a chasm and I need to become smarter if I'm going to successfully bridge it. I must not let Parkinson's steal my self-esteem.

*

I've been procrastinating over telling my father my news. Another day has passed since my visit to the neurologist and I know that I can't put it off any longer.

Since my mother died of cancer Dad and I have become very close. I'm proud of the way he looks after himself. He cooks and cleans his small unit and continues to be an amazing dad and grandad to us all. It's a lonely life when you lose your soul mate and I know he depends on me, sometimes just for being there. To have somebody to chat with over coffee, to share special moments, to go shopping with or to go on fun road trips. These things are hugely important.

Mary and Me

It was Dad's sister who spent the last years of her life in a rest home, suffering from late progression Parkinson's disease. Seeing her like that was heart-breaking and Dad found visiting hard. To now tell him his daughter has the same disease will not be easy.

I pull up in his driveway and give a cursory knock as I enter.

"Coffee on?" I walk over and plant a kiss on his cheek.

"I thought you'd be coming for coffee, so I've got it ready to brew."

"I can do that for you." I turn towards the kitchen.

"No, I'll do it. You take a seat."

I obediently find a seat and feel the tension release as I recognise the strong independent spirit that has been passed down from father to daughter.

From the kitchen he says, "I'm glad you dropped in today. I have something I want to show you."

"What's that, Dad?"

"I've made some real progress on the family tree I've been researching. Take a look at the pages on the table while I make the coffee."

Since losing Mum Dad's been researching our family tree and the more puzzles he's encountered the more enthusiastic he's become. I pick up the printouts and leaf through them. Each page has a table showing the details of a family. The top one has my parents' births, deaths and marriage dates as well the names of my two siblings and me and our birth and marriage dates. The second page has my grandparents' details and those of my parents' generation. The next page is for my great grandparents. And beyond that page are three more pages with dates suggesting they are a further three generations. Some of the early details appear sketchy with question marks in place of dates.

Dad comes back with a coffee cup in each hand and places them on the little table before disappearing back into the kitchen and reappearing with a plate of blueberry muffins, butter melting on the steaming halves.

"I made these this morning and think I've improved the recipe. I've increased the milk and I think they are a lighter texture than normal. What do you think?"

I select a muffin half and take a bite. "Mmm, this is good. Mum would be proud, or perhaps a little annoyed you are taking on her domain with such flare."

"Not likely."

I hold up the pages. "What's the new development in these?"

"Do you remember I had only managed to find information as far back as my great-grandparents' births, deaths and marriage details?"

I nod, mouth full of muffin.

"I've been in touch with the Hoxton Parish in London, trying to locate my great-great-grandparents. They've sent me the names and dates of my great-great-grandfather and his family. They go back to 1758."

"That's good progress, Dad." I wonder why it's so important to him to know his ancestry now when earlier in his life he'd shown little interest.

He reaches over to take the sheets of paper from me and flips to the back page. "See here, John, born 1758, married Mary, born 1761, and they had one child, Edward.

Edward must be my great-grandfather. The dates seem to fit."

"Good work."

"It's odd though. There's no recording of the date of death for my great-great-grandmother."

"It must be there somewhere. What about on the gravestones?"

"I don't know, but I'll send an email to the ancestry people and see what they suggest I do next."

We sit in silence, enjoying the coffee and muffins, comfortable in each other's company. I don't want to break the spell.

Finally, I say, "Dad, I had my appointment with the neurologist."

"Yes, I nearly forgot. How did it go?"

"Good. He was nice and put me through some tests."

"And?"

"He said I have Parkinson's disease." Those two little words again.

Dad stares at me, looking like I had hit him. "No! Oh Rose, I'm so sorry!"

"Not half as sorry as me," I say quietly, almost as a whisper.

He slumps back into his chair, looking shaken, and I glimpse the old man that he has become. His face is heavily wrinkled, his eyes watery. Age spots mar thinning skin that has a faint greyish hue. His posture is stooped. When did he get so old?

He continues to stare at me. "Aren't you too young to get that?"

"Apparently not." Tears well up in my eyes and I struggle to keep them contained.

"That's terrible news. I can't believe it." His eyes glisten with unfamiliar tears.

"That's how I feel."

I wait while he processes this news, trying to understand how it must feel to have a daughter with an old person's degenerative disease who could end up in nursing care, while their parent is still active and living independently. I fight back the tears and try to put the thoughts out of my mind. But then I remember Auntie Margaret looking helpless and pitiful in her wheelchair and I reach for a tissue and dab my eyes.

"Rose, you'll have to fight this. You can't give up, you must fight." His voice, weak and void of its usual oomph, betrays his feelings.

"Just as well you raised me to be stubborn." I smile at the memories of a wilful teenager.

"I don't know about that, but you are made of stern stuff." Normally he would have teased me about my bone-headedness, but today he just looks crestfallen. I haven't seen him like this since Mum lost her battle with cancer.

In this moment I know it is up to me to be strong and brave for all my family, my father included. Self-pity is a luxury that I cannot, will not entertain. I change the subject and we fall into our usual easy camaraderie as we chat about the vegetables in his allotment garden and the warrant of fitness needed for his car.

*

On my way home I decide to share my news with a couple of special friends who have been dealing with Parkinson's since Eric was diagnosed six or seven years ago. Eric was a colleague and mentor until his Parkinson's forced him into retirement. A quick call finds them home and eager for my visit.

It takes an hour to drive up the coast to Katikati and I welcome the time to chill and reflect on my current consulting project. I pull into their drive and walk the path to their door. I barely knock before it swings open and Tricia's beaming face greets me.

"How nice to see you." She pulls me into a warm hug.

"So glad you're home. How're you doing?"

"We're good. Eric's having a good day today. Go on through. He's in his usual chair."

Eric was up and coming towards me, his body shaking and writhing violently. "Hey Eric, you're looking good."

We hug, his thin frame bumps against my body as his tremors radiate out. This is us.

Eric offers coffee and moves into the kitchen. Tricia sits with me and we chat while Eric goes about making a pot of plunger coffee. I watch him as he shakily takes a scoop of ground coffee, only to spill granules all over the bench. His second attempt hits its mark. I look away and refocus on Tricia, embarrassed to witness his frustration.

Coffee made, Tricia gets up and helps Eric by carrying two mugs and hands one to me. I notice Eric has a different shaped mug with a straw in it.

As soon as we are seated, I say, "I have some news."

"What's that?" Tricia asks, eyes sparkling with genuine interest.

"I visited a second neurologist in Auckland and he said I have Parkinson's." Looking at Eric, I add, "I'm joining your club."

"I'm so very sorry." Tricia's face is etched in sympathy.

"Oh no, that's not good." His blank face is void of emotion.

"When Eric was diagnosed we knew little of the disease and weren't prepared for the speed it progressed. There are some things from our journey that you need to know." Tricia looked knowingly at Eric before carrying on. "Most importantly you need to rest lots. Eric has a nap every afternoon without fail. It's really important that you look after your body and get plenty of rest."

"I've never been an afternoon nap person. I don't like waking from a deep sleep, it makes me groggy." I take a biscuit from the plate being offered to me.

"Have you been prescribed any drugs?" Tricia asks.

"Yes, the specialist has prescribed a cocktail of three different types. I'm to start one at a time, ramping each one up very slowly before introducing the next one. We'll have to wait and see if they help with the tremor."

"Be aware of side effects. They can be nasty."

I want to say my neurologist said not to worry about side effects. Instead, I say, "I guess I'll deal with them if and when they come."

Tricia describes the trials and tribulations they've experienced with Eric's drugs. It has not been smooth sailing and there have been many adjustments to the drug regime over the years since he was first diagnosed. And some of the side effects experienced sound literally nightmarish. She describes how he would lash out in his sleep, hitting and kicking her, until they eventually agreed it would be safer if she slept in a separate bed.

Eric talks freely about his symptoms–how the tremor has progressed, the falls, the insomnia, the depression, his loss of voice power and the inability to do his beloved singing, constipation, apathy, muscle pain, hallucinations and so much more. My positive spirit gives way to uneasiness as I wonder how long until I'm like him.

Listening to them, the line between Parkinson's symptoms and the side effects of the drugs blurs and it's even more confusing. The drugs supposedly make the symptoms more bearable, but then the drugs can have side effects that look like the symptoms. I silently commit to doing my own research.

I leave Eric and Tricia's, feeling the full weight of the diagnosis.

Driving home I rub my head to ease the pounding in my temples. My eyes swim with tears that blur my vision and I call Gary, desperate to hear his encouraging words.

"Hi, what's up?" he asks.

"I've been to Dad's and broke the news and then called on Eric and Tricia. They've given me a reality check and I might as well slit my wrists now." It's a poor attempt at humour and perhaps there is more truth to it than I care to admit.

"Now babe, there's no place for negative talk. You know you have to stay positive."

"Yeah, I know. The future just seems so unbearably hard right now. I don't know if I can do this."

"Of course you can and you will. You're strong. I just don't want you to listen to any negative talk, especially if I'm not with you."

"Easily said. Tricia and Eric spoke the truth out of love for me, you know that. I'm just not ready to hear it."

"Your Parkinson's is our walk and no one else's. Let's just take it one step at a time. I'll be home soon and we can talk about it then. In the meantime, stay positive. Just because you have the diagnosis doesn't mean you are any sicker than last week. We'll fight this thing together."

We say our good-byes and I hang up and turn on the radio to find some upbeat music.

The music does nothing to suppress my feeling of impending doom, not even when the station plays Billy Joel's *The Stranger*, a favourite from university days, which normally brings a smile to my face.

We all have faces that we hide away forever. And we take them out and show ourselves when everyone has gone. Some are satin, some are steel, some are silk, and some are leather. They're the faces of a stranger but we'd love to try them on.

Margaret's face became expressionless. Will I too wear a mask of steel? I let my tears flow unchecked. They stream down my cheeks making driving difficult, but I don't care.

Why me? Why now? These questions circle in my mind like a shark circling its prey. We have been so full of hope for our future. We've saved hard so we can have a retirement doing the things we've always dreamed of and now those dreams are smashed. This disease will rob us of our future and that is so unfair, for Gary as well as me. I will become a burden, something he hadn't signed on for.

My tremor escalates as my stress builds. My left hand barely stays on the wheel and my left knee shakes uncontrollably. Even though my driving ability isn't impaired, I grip the wheel even harder and pull into our drive. From somewhere deep inside I muster some grit. I must cope with this new reality. I simply have no options. I wipe the tears away with the back of my hand and get out of the car and enter the house.

With Eric still on my mind, I decide to start my exercise programme today with a walk. Our house is on the side of a steep hill that overlooks the harbour, so no matter which way you walk there's always a hill to climb. It's been some time since I've done any walking as I keep using the excuse of being injured.

As I change into some walking-type clothes and appropriate shoes my body feels particularly tired and heavy, screaming at me to rest. I almost change my mind, opting to find some emails to answer instead. I force myself to go out the door, knowing I need it more than ever to overcome the apathy.

Ten minutes into the walk I'm on the steepest part of the slope and my lungs heave. My legs start to feel lethargic and I become light headed. Not that long ago I was reasonably fit from playing squash, but lately I've been out with injuries and my body has quickly lost its fitness. I decide to walk just the short block. In less than twenty minutes I'm walking back up the drive.

*

For the rest of the afternoon I busy myself with household chores, not wanting to dwell on our uncertain future. Part of me wants to punish my body for its betrayal. How long do I have before the physical symptoms prevent me from doing the things I love? Things like travel, sailing, going for a trek in the bush and my work.

Gary comes home at the usual time and I can sense he too is preoccupied.

"We need to talk," I say.

"About what?" He comes over and pecks me on the cheek.

"Our future." I follow him into the study where he drops off his briefcase.

"Do we really need to talk about it? It won't do any good."

"I do. You know I need to talk and get the big stuff out. I need help processing."

"How about I pour us a drink first?" he asks.

Not needing an answer he goes to the fridge and pulls out a beer and a bottle of Pinot Gris. While he pours I fix us a plate of crackers and cheese. We take them to the lounge.

"Cheers—to us!" He raises his bottle in the customary toast.

"To us!" I return the toast and raise the glass to my lips. The cold liquid is an elixir. I roll it about my mouth, enjoying the crisp taste of fruit with a hint of spice.

"So, what is it you want to talk about?" he asks.

"I've been thinking about how long I'll be able to manage my consulting business and board work. There's also the trip to Kenya coming up. Should we be thinking about cancelling that?"

"Why would you want to give them up?"

"What if I'm working at a less than full cognitive level? That's not fair on my clients or my colleagues."

He laughs. "You're a long way off that."

His confidence is irritating and my voice has a slight edge to it as I retort, "How can you possibly know that?"

He looks at me with a gentle expression and says in a low voice, "Trust me, I'll know when you change. Right now, it's not an issue."

I take a deep sip of the wine, allowing the liquid to sooth my nerves.

Gary continues. "I thought increased exercise and reduced stress were called for. It seems to me the logical thing might be to give up your consulting work. That would give you the time you need and would help avoid undue stress."

"But if I stop my consulting, my cognitive decline could be more rapid. If you don't use it, you lose it, right?"

"True. But by giving up your consulting you reduce stress, gain time for exercise and you can still do your writing to keep the brain going. At least that's at your own pace with no pressure."

"Can we afford for me to stop?" I toy with the sleek stem of the elegant wine glass. "Won't it impact our retirement plans?"

"Try not to look too far ahead."

"Easy to say …" Tears form and I look away, wanting to be strong, for both of us.

But he knows me too well and his hand brushes my cheek. "Let's not get ahead of ourselves and instead focus on what we can do now." His voice is full of emotion. "I'm not ready to think too far ahead. As far as money goes, we'll adjust. That's the benefit of having worked hard and saved while we could."

I turn to look at this man with whom I've shared my life, who promised to love me through sickness and health and who I know would make that promise again, even knowing what we now know.

"Maybe you're right. If I'm going to get serious about daily exercise then I need to make time for it. And it's hard to manage my time when working for clients as it can be a feast or a famine. If we can afford it maybe it is time to hang up the briefcase."

"I think that's really important. If you are happy to give it up, we can live without the income. I want you to focus on being well. That's more important than dollars."

"What about the charitable board work?"

"You could consider giving up the board chair position and perhaps just stay on as a board member for now. Maybe also give up some of your committee roles that take more of your time."

"I've been thinking it's time to hand over the role of delegate to the congress as we need to spread it around the board more. I could also stand down from my congressional committees. And I agree about the chair's role. It can only be good for the organisation to have some new blood in the chair."

"Are you sure you want to do that?" Gary studies me intently.

"I don't know, I do love it. It's a new reality that we are dealing with and I guess I should step down from some commitments. I just wish I knew what the future is going to look like—how much time I have while I can still function well."

"I think it's best we don't know. Anyway, because you love it you should keep your hand in, at least for now. There's really no urgency to make changes so long as you're avoiding excessive stress and putting effort into exercise."

"Yeah, maybe so. What about the congress in Kenya? The bookings are all made and they're not refundable." I pause and, thinking aloud, add, "It will be a chance to say my goodbyes. And I've been really looking forward to our East African holiday. It could be our last overseas adventure. Although, I'm worried about how my body will cope with the travel."

Since being confirmed as the New Zealand delegate to the congress, we'd decided to turn it into a holiday. I'm booked to go on ahead to take part in the week-long congress near Nairobi and at the end of the week Gary is booked to join me. From Nairobi we will fly to the Maasai Mara for a wildlife safari and then to Kampala in Uganda, to spend time with friends. Our travels will take us to the north and south of the country and we'll visit the Uganda projects. All our flights, accommodation and safari holidays were reserved long before my diagnosis.

"There's no reason why you shouldn't go. You're up to the travel. The holiday will do us good and it may not even be our last. Does it matter? Let's just go and have a great time regardless of health issues. We'll probably never get the opportunity to visit East Africa again."

"You're right. It is the holiday of a lifetime."

I take another sip of my wine and we sit in silence. My eyes focus on the bookshelf full of photo albums and photobooks. Photography has been a hobby for me and an important part of my life. I studied black and white when working in the United Kingdom and we'd even built a darkroom into our previous house. A sadness settles over me like a shadow as I consider how hard it is to hold a camera steady.

"You might have to take the photos," I say, interrupting the silence. "I could tell you how to compose the shot and what settings to use."

Gary laughs, a little too loudly. "That would turn you into the travelling companion from hell. Can you imagine how frustrated you would be with me and my ineptness to take good photos? No, you'll just have to use your tripod."

My left side starts to shake more and I clench my jaws. "But that's not practical when travelling. How can it be? How can I be in a Land Rover with other tourists and have a tripod set up? And what about the time it would take to set it up whenever I want to photograph an animal. The moment would pass before I get anywhere close to releasing the shutter."

"Does it really matter? Maybe you need to just enjoy the experience and not worry about photos."

Why can't he see how important this is to me? My frustration turns into anger and it's reflected in my voice. "But photography is part of me, it's in my DNA."

"Then either you find a way to steady the camera or I take some snaps for our memory, but don't ask me to take award winning photos."

I look him in the eye, ashamed of my outburst. "I'm sorry. I just feel so frustrated that this disease is robbing me of the things I love."

It would be unbearable to hand my camera over and not to take the photos myself, especially since I find making good compositions extremely satisfying. Travel photography requires steady hands as the scene is often dynamic, either while shooting from a moving vehicle or because subjects are moving and not posed. Camera shake does not make for sharp photos. I think of sports photographers lined up at the side of a rugby field with cameras resting on monopods. Eureka!

"I've an idea," I say, a glimmer of hope drawing me out of my gloom. "I could use a monopod, you know, like a sports photographer."

"That's a great idea." His voice is full of enthusiasm. "You should look into it tomorrow. I would love to see you carrying on with your photography."

"And I could experiment with faster shutter speeds and higher ISO settings. Perhaps I can minimise the effect of the tremor." I talk quickly, excited at the possibility of finding a solution to the problem.

"Now that sounds more like the woman I married." He raises his beer. "To you, my intrepid photographer. May you create many more stunning compositions."

His wide grin is contagious and I beam in response. "To us." I raise my wine glass. "And to our African adventure. Perhaps we've saved our best holiday adventure to the last." I down the remaining wine in one last mouthful.

"Or perhaps there are still more to come," he corrects me.

4

Rose, Tauranga, February 2017

I walk into the community centre with nervous anticipation for the official launch of my debut novel. It's been a long time in the making and I can't wait to share this moment with our friends and family. To have a novel published has been a life goal, pushing me well outside my work and life experience and it's been quite a journey to get to this point.

The novel was inspired by an experience that had impacted my life. As a young graduate I travelled to the United Kingdom for a gap year and worked as a live-in au pair for a family in north London. In the following June I took a week off and headed for Lesmahagow, a small town in Scotland where my grandmother was born. One afternoon, when walking along an abandoned railway track looking for a place to take a photo, a stranger jumped me and attempted to strangle me.

Although I managed to escape with minor injuries—bruises and abrasions that would fully heal—the fear was overwhelming. While I couldn't change what happened to me I learned I could control my response to it and soon discovered some coping strategies that helped me overcome the fear so I could get on with my life.

One of those strategies was to force myself to focus on the positives that came out of the experience. Although they were hard to find, there were a few. It had given me an opportunity to learn more about my character, things many of us never find out. I realised that if subjected to terror I'm likely to experience delayed shock, which will allow me to face the immediate situation rationally. I also believed I was extraordinarily lucky to have lived through it and the chances of it ever happening twice in a lifetime must be extremely low. Perhaps foolishly, I set about putting myself in risky situations to prove it—not something I would advise anyone else to do, but it worked for me and I regained confidence and some freedom over my emotions and my life.

At the time, sharing my story with others helped. The more I talked about it the more I felt distanced from the experience, as if it had happened to someone else and I was just relating the story. My brain gradually blocked out some of the hurtful memories, such as his face and his name. I also picked up the habit of positive self-talk and became very good at telling myself I could do things when I lacked confidence.

My creative writing journey began a couple of years ago, using the assault as the central theme. In the beginning my motivation was to share it with my family so they would understand more about what I'd been through. The drive to write that story became more than just relating what had happened to me. It was another way of turning the experience into something positive.

Writing it had been therapeutic. I had gained some closure from subsequent visits to Lesmahagow and writing this book has really helped seal that chapter of my life. There's a real sense of freedom in expressing deeply-held feelings and it's empowering to take control over the ending by writing the outcome I always wanted but never got. I've been able to say things to my assailant that I never had the opportunity to say in real life, mainly because I haven't seen him since that afternoon.

Now after what has turned out to be a marathon journey, my novel is published and about to be launched.

Scanning the hall I notice the chairs have been arranged neatly around the perimeter and there's a table for drinks and platters of food. Gary and Michael enter carrying cartons of glasses and stack them in the corner.

"Hey Mum." Michael comes over and gives me a hug. "You must be excited to finally launch the book."

"Sure am."

They head back out for another load.

The boxes of precious books are under a table. I pull some out and carefully display them, leaving space on the table where I can autograph copies. It's all a bit surreal. Two years ago I would have laughed at the thought of being at a book launch, signing copies of my own novel.

Soon everything is ready and my friends start arriving. An excited buzz grows as more people arrive. I stand near the door to welcome them, many of whom encouraged me to complete the book and have it published. I owe them so much.

As I chat with friends, the shadow of my diagnosis hangs over me and prevents me from fully revelling in the thrill of the occasion. It's foremost in my mind. The tremor does not let me forget.

Mary and Me

My brother Pete walks in and I greet him with a hug.

"How're you doing, Sis?"

"Great, thanks." I look at him and add, "Actually not so great. Has Dad talked to you?"

"What about?"

"I have some not so good news. I went to a neurologist and he said I have Parkinson's disease." There it was again, those two words that cause so much devastation.

"What? Really? Wow, that sucks."

"Yep, sure does." My eyes well up with tears.

"I'm so sorry, Sis." He looks at me and I recognise a look of pity on his face. "So, what's the prognosis?"

I swallow hard, trying to keep it together. "Let's talk after tonight. I can't just now. Let's meet for coffee sometime soon."

He nods. "Sure, but that's a real bummer. By the way, congratulations on the book launch. Good effort."

"Thanks, it's been quite a journey. I'll catch you later."

"You'll be all right, you always are." He looks away as if hiding the tears that fill his eyes.

"Mmm, that's what everyone keeps telling me. I want to believe it." My voice has that tell-tale quiver. His obvious struggle to contain his emotions makes me battle to stifle my own tears.

I look around to see the crowd now filling the hall. "Hey, I need to keep mingling."

Pete takes me by surprise and gives me an extra hug. Sympathy and pity are hard pills to swallow. Tears well up and this time they overflow. I turn away so he can't see them and pull a tissue out of my bag, carefully dabbing it around my eyes, trying not to smudge my mascara.

A hand lightly touches my arm and I turn to see Dad. "How're you feeling?"

"Good. Excited about finally launching the book." I give him a hug.

"Congratulations! I have to admit I thought you were mad when you first told me you were writing a novel, but you did it."

I laugh. "Only my bone-headedness got me through and I believe I've got you to thank for that."

Dad smiles. "I'm not so sure about that. By the way, I have some more news. The ancestry outfit in the UK have found an old will that appears to be my great-great-grandfather's. There's no mention of his wife and he left everything to his only child, my great-grandfather. It gave us some new information. His occupation was apparently a confectioner."

"Interesting. Perhaps that's where my sweet tooth comes from."

My cousin Robert and his wife Anna make a beeline for us. They greet me with kisses on both cheeks and shake hands with my dad, who excuses himself to join my brother.

"Hey Cuz, how're things?" Robert asks.

I try to sound bright. "Great. So glad you could come."

"It's good that you gave us an invite. Congratulations on your book. You must be feeling excited." Anna says.

"Thanks and yes I am excited. This has been a long time coming." My left hand is shaking badly and I know

I should tell them. "There's something I think you should know. I've been diagnosed with Parkinson's disease."

"What?" Robert's jaw drops and his mouth is open.

Tears well up again and I mop them up with the damp tissue.

"Yep, it's still a shock."

Margaret's thin, useless body lying in that awful bed chair comes to mind, her eyes silently pleading with me.

I lower my voice. "I keep thinking about your Mum."

"Gawd, that's terrible." Robert continues to look crestfallen. "When did you find out?"

"A week ago. It's still a bit raw."

"Poor you." Robert frowns and I recognise the pity in his eyes.

"Rose, I'm so sorry." Anna speaks quietly in a voice that's full of concern.

More tears and probably more smudges.

"Help yourselves to a drink and snack." I point to the table in the corner. "And I'll see you later." I try to give my best smile, but I'm not feeling overly brave.

My emotions teeter on the edge. I can deal with it until I become the object of pity and then I fall apart. I have to keep it together. This is a night of celebration, not a pity party. The toilets offer sanctuary and a place to restore my resolve. I hurry past some friends with a quick, "Back in a minute." I take my time to brush my hair and get rid of the smudges that have formed around my eyes.

The girls from my squash team spot me as I walk back in and they head straight for me.

"Congratulations!" "How does it feel?" "Well done you." "Wow, you're an author!" "I know someone famous!"

It all comes as a chorus—Sophie, Debs, Natalie, Cheryl, Janine. Their faces grin generously.

Their enthusiasm is contagious and I laugh with them. "Thanks, team."

"How are you feeling?" Sophie asks.

"Pretty pleased with myself. And thank you for your encouragement. I'm not sure I would have finished the book if it wasn't for you."

Sophie had read my early draft and was one of the friends who encouraged me to keep writing and take the manuscript to a publisher.

"No worries. I think you should be very proud of your effort."

"Thanks."

"How's the injury?" Debs asks. "Are you coming back to squash anytime soon?"

"I'm keen to try as soon as I get on top of my shoulder injury. It's still frozen and I can't lift my arm above the shoulder. It just doesn't seem to be getting any better. I've had another cortisone injection, but it hasn't really worked." I pause and smile at them. "I miss the team and don't know when I'll be able to get back on the court. I'm not doing any exercise at the minute and am rapidly going down a deep sloth hole."

"You'll come right. Just give it time." Janine sounds more cheerful than I feel.

"I hope so. Right now I can't even put my hands behind my back to do up my bra strap and sometimes I need help to pull a T-shirt over my head."

"Are you going to physio?" Janine asks.

"Yes, but so far it doesn't seem to be helping much. I'm over being injured. It's been nearly two years of frozen shoulders and pain."

"You'll have to get it right in time to train for the eliminations tournament," Natalie adds.

"I'll be disappointed if I have to miss it—it's so much fun. It must be our turn to take the trophy. I just don't think I'm going to be up for it this year." I look at my friends and am compelled to share my news with them. "I've just found out I have Parkinson's disease."

"What?" I look at the stunned faces looking at me, eyes wide, mouths open.

"Yeah, it's a blow."

"Oh Rose, I'm so sorry." I'm virtually passed from one to another as they hug me and utter how sorry they are to hear my news. Condolences. How appropriate given that something inside of me seems to have died. Never again can I take my health for granted. Becoming disabled freaks me out and I choke back my tears.

"When did you find out?"

"Just a week ago. It explains my tremor and rigidity and how sometimes I can't seem to raise myself out of an intense feeling of apathy. I've been struggling to find enough energy on court, even before my latest injury when I was relatively fit. It made it hard for me to get into the game. I now think that might have been the Parkinson's."

"This is such awful news." Sophie says.

I start to tear up again. "Yep, but let's not talk about it tonight. Help yourselves to drinks and something to eat. I had better meet some of the other guests."

I mingle among friends, making a real effort to put on my happy face and to ignore the tremor. The room is full of chatter and the sound of clinking glasses. Writing my first novel was a monumental effort that used a whole new set of skills. To now have it published is worthy of celebration and I should be revelling in it and not allowing my diagnosis to ruin my evening.

Then it dawns on me that my tremor was already persistent when I began writing the book, although I was blissfully ignorant of the disease lurking in my brain. Put that way, it's an even bigger achievement. I smile and pick up a glass of wine from a tray being offered. This is my night and, Parkinson's or not, I am going to enjoy it. *So, take that Parkinson's!*

Lance, our MC for the evening, calls everyone to attention. Gerald, representing the publisher, gets up and shares a few words about my book journey. Then it's my turn. I look around the faces of my family and friends and see genuine smiles, not pity. This is about my book launch, not Parkinson's. That can wait.

I begin with an outline of the plot. I explain that the book is about a young woman on her gap year who visits the town where her grandmother came from. While there, she's violently attacked by a stranger. The story relates how this traumatic episode impacts both of their lives. I tell them it's a story primarily of forgiveness, fear and guilt as well as the coping strategies for recovering from a trauma. The main character shares some of my own experiences, but she's not me.

I tell them how, when writing the story through her eyes, I became more and more curious about what would drive a stranger to attack a woman and what impact the guilt would have on his life. This led to the development of her attacker's character who is entirely fictitious. I have no idea who my real assailant was nor what became of him.

I compare my writing journey to running a marathon; how it began as a story for the family, then grew into a novel. I told them how I read the first chapter to Gary, who tactfully suggested a creative writing course. This gets a laugh.

I outline the strategies that helped me overcome my fear and break through the emotional paralysis that followed the trauma. The one thing in my control was my response to the assault, which led me to look for ways to transform my negative experience into something positive. I mention how I refused to be a victim and was determined not to let it define me.

As I speak, a peace settles over me. It is as if a bookmark hangs in the air, a truth that needs exploring, a parallel path I need to walk. I focus back on my talk.

I end by saying if just one person takes encouragement and strength from my story then everything has been worthwhile. By everything, I mean even the assault itself. Good will come out of bad if we allow it.

As I finish my speech to a round of applause, Gary stands up unexpectedly and comes over to my side.

"I'm so proud of my wife and what she's achieved," he says.

Never good at receiving praise, I feel the heat rushing into my cheeks and I barely hear the rest. My eyes fill and I blink the tears away.

More applause.

With the formal part of the evening over, I am showered with hugs and congratulations before being propelled over to the table where copies of my books are laid out. A small queue waits for me to sign their newly-purchased books. I sit down and start to write. The pen shakes wildly in my left hand and I flex my fingers to try and still the tremor.

I've lost sleep worrying about my inability to write legibly in the books, so much so that I practised the inscription over and over until I could manage something that was a little more than child-like. I hate that I can't make the writing neat when I've worked so hard on the completed narrative in the book. I find myself continually apologising for my scrawl, but no one seems to mind, that is, no one but me.

Brian approaches the table and picks up a copy of my book. He passes it to me and I open the cover to sign it. Having signed so many already, my tremor is now worse and it takes concentration to get the pen onto the page to start the inscription.

"I see you have a tremor," he says.

I smile and nod, not wishing to discuss it with the husband of my friend, Fran.

"Is it Parkinson's?" he continues. Then before I get a chance to answer, he adds, "My father had it. A horrible condition."

"Yes, it's Parkinson's."

"You poor thing. It's an awful downhill slide, just awful."

I resent his tone and his pity. "I intend to fight it."

Mary and Me

He looks at me, eyebrows rising over the top of his glasses. "You can't beat it, there's no point fighting. You just have to accept it." He pauses. "You know it's got you, got you for life."

I hold his gaze. Then in my calmest voice I say, "As long as I have breath, I have hope."

The pile of books slowly disappears and the signing is over. A glass of wine is thrust into my hand by a grinning husband and it's time to forget my fears and just bask in the moment. Having Parkinson's somehow makes the celebration even sweeter.

*

I waken to intense pain. In a single movement I grab my foot and pull it up, flexing it, panting with the familiar pain of cramp. This time it's my calf muscle. At other times it can be my feet that cramp causing me to physically uncurl the toes.

"What is it?" Gary murmurs sleepily.

"Nothing, just cramp, sorry." The pain eases and I lie back down.

Cramps seem to be happening with increasing regularity and I make a mental note to add magnesium to my growing list of supplements.

The sound of slow, rhythmic breathing fills the darkness and I'm aware Gary has already returned to his dreams. Sleep comes easily to him and I envy him that, even though it was not long ago that I too would sleep through the nights. This nightly ritual of waking in the wee hours, with or without cramps, happens regardless of how tired I might be when I turn off the light.

It's still dark when I open my eyes to peer at the time glowing from the clock on the bedside table. Two fifteen a.m. Again. I sigh with frustration and turn over, snuggling further under the covers. I try willing myself to sleep.

I don't allow myself any stimulation so as not to encourage the habit. I've always thought it's like training a baby to sleep through the night. If you stimulate them when they wake with play and chatter they will wake expecting to play every night. If I allow myself to get up and read, then it's a reward for waking up. I lie in the dark, desperately holding on to positive thoughts, constructive plans. Seconds, minutes, then hours tick by.

Things are always bleaker in the early morning hours. Parkinson's is much scarier, our future is more uncertain and the unknowns are an unfathomable void. The events since hearing those two words spoken over me whirl about my head. A kaleidoscope of memories. A fusillade of thoughts. Something niggles, something stored to explore further.

My body is weak, my limbs feel strange and faintly tingly, as if wrapped in tight socks. And yet I know they are bare between the sheets. My tremor reminds me that I'm awake and I heave my body over to my other side, curling up into the foetal position.

The book launch comes to mind. Writing the novel was an epic achievement and I wonder if I have another book in me. I've started to receive positive feedback. People love to read a story about real life situations and my story was about forgiveness and positivity. Positivity inspires hope.

The main lesson I learned when assaulted all those years ago was that traumatic events may not be in your control, but your response is. The same must be true for having an incurable disease. Such a simple concept and yet it can be so easily overlooked, especially when feeling devastated by the change and fear a diagnosis brings. When I took control and overcame the fear that followed my attack I worked hard to focus on the positives. And now I need to find the positives in having Parkinson's disease.

A picture of Margaret forms in my mind and I'm overwhelmed by fear. I don't want to end my days as she did. And I'm so much younger than she was when she was diagnosed. I become unbearably hot and damp between the sheets and I push them away in a desperate attempt to cool down. I'm so very scared.

Fear. It's penetrating my life. Again. I need to keep my brain busy to keep the fear from overwhelming me. What is it that I fear most? Is it the fear of ending up like Margaret? Is it fear of becoming a burden? Is it fear of losing control over my life? Is it fear of the unknown? Maybe it's all of these.

I need to be positive. I will not let Parkinson's define me. It might be a thorn in my side that I have to live with, but it will not change me. I am still me.

I pray for wisdom, strength and courage to face my new adversary, this disease of mine.

My mind drifts to our holiday in Africa. It is only days away now and I'm starting to get excited. I make a mental list of all the things I need to do to prepare for the trip. It's like counting sheep.

The shrill sound of the alarm wakes me up. The light is shining around the curtain and I realise I've been sleeping.

5

Mary, London, 1804

Mary rises before the dawn, drawing her shawl around her shoulders while taking care not to wake John. He seldom rouses in good humour if woken from a deep slumber. She says a short prayer, thankful for his deep snores. While the harshest months of winter are past the early mornings are still cold and dark. The wick of the candle sparks into light as she touches it to an ember in the fireplace, filling the room with a warm glow and casting shadows on the walls.

She tiptoes over to the porcelain jug and basin and washes herself, working quickly so as not to be caught in a state of undress by her husband. Her clothes are laid out from the night before and she pulls on the chemise that was drying in front of the hearth. Over that she puts on her grey woollen work dress and apron. The cold sends a shiver through her and she quickly wraps a woollen shawl around her shoulders. It takes time to comb out her long fair tresses until they feel silky, a task she loves to do. She crowns them with a linen cap.

Taking care to avoid the creaky floorboards she tiptoes out of the bedroom, holding her skirt in one hand and the candle in the other. As she descends the narrow stairs the candle flickers as the lantern trembles and she drops the skirt to steady it with her other hand. She stumbles on the bottom stair as her foot catches the hem and she barely manages to stay on her feet. She silently berates herself for her clumsiness.

The kitchen is a small room in the back of the shop, doubling as the factory where the sweets are made. An empty cream container sits on the floor beside the wooden bench. She picks it up and hurries out the door. The early morning air is still, the light from the lamps eerie amid the wisps of fog rising from the river. Even so, the streets are already teeming with women going about their chores and labourers on their way to the workhouses. She navigates the cobbles, avoiding horse manure and other rubbish. Nearing the marketplace she jostles her way through the crowd to buy cream from the back of a cart and walks hurriedly back to the shop, eager to be home before John rises.

The excursion wearies her and she's relieved to put the cream can down. The embers in the hearth show no life as she clears away the ash and sets a fire with a little paper and kindling. She lights it with the candle just as muffled voices can be heard above and floorboards creak with light footsteps.

In the fireplace hang two large cauldrons, each blackened from years of sweet making. She takes one off its hook and carries it to the work bench. Red welts from burns mar the back of each hand and she studies them in the candlelight. Of late she has been unusually clumsy, frequently burning herself with the hot syrup during sweet making. She will need to take more care.

"Good mornin', mother-in-law," Florence says.

Mary and Me

Mary looks around to see her daughter-in-law enter with baby Mildred in her arms and Henry holding on to her skirt. She is a hearty woman, with a round and rosy face framed in a mass of mouse-brown ringlets that escape her lace cap.

"Good mornin', Florence. Good mornin', me sweet cherubs." Mary moves across and affectionately kisses the children on their foreheads.

"Shall I measure them ingredients for the first batch of sweets?" Florence asks, unwrapping the shawl from around Mildred and spreading it on the floor before lying her down. Henry, his little chubby face partially obscured by his stack of dishevelled brown curls, stays clinging to her skirt.

"Thank you, Florence." She finds Florence's help to be a blessing especially with this weariness that lately has become her constant companion, something she has been unable to shake off. A visit to the apothecary to seek a sleep remedy might be worthwhile.

Florence hums a simple tune as she works. Her buxom figure swells under her brown work dress and apron, hinting at another babe on the way. She hasn't said anything but Mary can tell. Her own pregnancies resulted in only one surviving child—Edward, Florence's husband. This has long been a disappointment to John who'd expected to have many offspring, just as his mother had produced for his father.

Mary busies herself with the oatmeal. Heavy footsteps overhead cause her to pause and she exchanges glances with Florence before returning her attention to the pot she is stirring. The fire burns hot in the hearth and she swelters in its heat, her burns raw.

"Best 'ave that gruel ready." Florence places the plates and spoons on the table.

John's large figure appears at the foot of the stairs in his undergarments, his long pasty face looking troubled under the shadow of stubble.

He gives Mary a hard look. "Where's me clothes, woman?"

"Yer clothes are over the back of the chair. If it pleases you, I can shave you after breakfast."

John grunts and turns back towards the stairs, just as a second set of footsteps hasten down the stairs behind him. Edward is a younger version of his father; tall and solid in build, but not yet growing the belly. Thankfully, his is a more agreeable disposition. Even though cursed with fair hair that is wild and woolly he looks a gentleman in brown breeches, stockings and with a fitting waistcoat over his shirt.

John, now dressed in a white shirt and breeches, reappears and Florence brings the pot of gruel over to the table. As she ladles it into plates, Mary adds the cream. They sit around the table with John at the head, Edward with Henry beside him, Florence with Mildred on her lap opposite, and Mary. They wait for John to say the grace.

After the grace John picks up his spoon, signalling they can eat.

Mary passes the loaf of white bread to John, who breaks some off and uses it to scoop up a mouthful of the gruel.

Mary and Me

Henry plays with a crust. His constant jabbering causes Mary to glance nervously at Florence.

"Shhh," Edward chides him, to no avail.

"Children should be seen and not 'eard." John looks darkly at Edward.

Edward's voice is soft as he answers, "'E's just a baby and doesn't yet understand."

"Never too young to be taught," John retorts. "He'll be better for it in the end."

Edward spoons gruel into Henry's mouth and his chattering stops while he concentrates on his food. Florence eats quickly and is the first to excuse herself from the table.

"You see to the nippers, Florence," Mary says. "I can clear up down 'ere."

Florence shoots her a grateful look and, with Mildred on her hip, takes Henry by the hand and leads him upstairs.

Mary finishes her breakfast and begins to clear the table. As she carries a load to the sink, plates crash and she stands amid pieces of broken crockery.

"Woman!" John's voice booms into the empty spaces around the room. "What on earth?"

Stunned and unsure how it happened she sinks to her knees and tears well up in her eyes. "So so sorry," she stutters. "I know not what came over me."

Her left hand trembles badly as she picks up the pieces and she can't make it stop. Instinctively she moves her body to hide it from John's line of sight. She weeps silently, unsure how it happened. She never used to be this ungainly.

After cleaning up the mess, she finishes clearing the table and the rest of the morning passes without further incident. John, clean shaven and dressed in his coat and hat, stands outside the shop passing the time with neighbouring shopkeepers and passers-by. Edward mans the shop and, during the quiet times, joins the men congregating outside. Nothing more is said about the broken crockery.

Florence helps Mary with the sugary treats while minding the little ones. The ingredients are mixed and boiled in pots over the fire before being poured into lined trays to cool. One tray is cut into small rectangles that are twisted and left to harden. Another is cut into interesting shapes and dusted with fine sugar. Brittle candy is smashed into pieces with the little silver hammer and chisel. Restocked jars covered with round paper tops are added to the shelves around the counter, creating neat rows displaying an appetising array of boiled sweets, marzipan, preserved fruit, gingerbread, sugared almonds and biscuits.

"Them treats look good enough to eat." Mary studies the jars. "Just look at them colours and shapes."

"It's rightly colourful and should lead even the thriftiest of customers into temptation." Edward beams at his mother.

"Let's 'ope so," says John coming into the shop. "'Tis a quiet mornin'."

"It'll pick up," Mary says.

Florence stands with her baby on one hip and hand on the other, eyeing Edward. "It'll do us no good standing 'ere when there's work to be done."

The way she says it makes Mary wonder if the words are directed at her. Henry begins to grizzle and toddles towards Mary, his little arms reaching upwards. She swoops down, picks him up and rocks him.

"This poor lad is tired, Florence. Do you want to take the nippers up while I finish down 'ere?" Mary asks.

"Are you sure you don't mind?"

"Of course not. Away with you now."

Edward plants a kiss on Henry's forehead and Florence takes the children upstairs. Mary sighs deeply and turns back to the kitchen where she scrubs the dishes, surfaces and lastly the floor. When the manual work is done she picks up the heavy ledger from its place on the counter and carries it to the table. This is her favourite time of day, a time of peace when she can sit and update the accounts.

Opening the ledger to the current page she studies with pride the neat columns of numbers drawn in her own hand. Her mother taught her to read and write as well as how to add and subtract columns of numbers. She loved learning, never able to get enough. At the time, neither mother nor daughter had any idea what a gift it would be. Like her mother had taught her, she'd taught Edward the books. While quick with numbers he now prefers to handle the money and spend time in the company of men.

She looks towards the shop front and sees John holding court with a small group of men. Some of them are neighbours and she is in no doubt that John will be sharing his opinions of politics and commerce, as men are in the habit of doing. In the early days of their marriage she sought to share her views, but she soon learned that he viewed her incapable of having an opinion on such matters and so she gave up trying.

When she was young and foolish she'd imagined marrying for love. It was a fancy notion and many a girl's dream, although few found it. John is not a bad man and yet he doesn't see her, really see her. He sees only the woman who bore and raised his child, cooks his meals and cleans house, the woman who stocks the shelves and keeps the books. Sometimes she thinks he's forgotten just how much she has helped him grow his business. Things could be a lot worse, however, and she is lucky that she doesn't have to put up with the beatings that many women endure at the hands of their men. She is well fed and clothed, and has her family and this shop. There is no reason to complain.

She dips the nib into the ink pot and is about to start writing when her thumb gets a strange and barely noticeable twitch. It seems to move of its own accord. She flexes her fingers, and it stops. When she holds her hands out in front of her it restarts. Strange.

A bell jangles as the door to the shop opens and a woman comes in with two small children. Edward is there to serve them. Mary turns her attention back to the bookkeeping.

Carefully, she writes numbers in the columns, blotting the ink as she goes. Today it is more difficult to make the numerals consistently round and neat, something she has only recently noticed. She turns back the pages to compare her work. What was once a beautiful script has over time been getting ever so slightly smaller and less round. It is a strange thing, but a pattern nevertheless and it would be best to hide this from John. Thinking how easy it will be to keep it from him makes her smile. For all his bluster, he is not a numbers man and leaves that part of the business to Edward and her. With extra care, taking time to make her strokes neat, she completes the work and softly closes the ledger.

*

Mary picks up her wicker basket and wraps the shawl more snuggly around her shoulders. "I be off now, Florence."

John and Edward are at the counter talking with a customer, one of the regulars.

"Good afternoon, Mary." The lady beams a wide smile, showing several gaps where teeth had once been. Four of her young ones run around her skirts, giggling and jabbing one another.

Mary smiles, thinking how much John loathes unruliness. "Good afternoon to you, Alice. A mighty fine day today."

"A fine day indeed."

"Might I recommend the twists. They be particularly good today, even though I say so meself."

"Your treats are the best this side of the Thames, make no mistake. 'Tis worth me walk up the 'ill. Ain't they, children?"

The children, ignoring her, continue their game of mayhem.

"Will that be all?" John asks.

"Better add a dozen of 'em twists." She smiles at Mary.

Taking a small sheet of paper Edward expertly rolls it on the diagonal to make a cone, then fills it with the sweets and closes it with a swift turn at the top. John collects the coins offered and Edward passes the cones to Alice who puts them in her basket, provoking a chorus of protests from her children.

"Good day." She glides out the door, her children in tow still complaining.

"Give me some coin, will you John? We be needing some more ingredients."

John opens the wooden box kept under the counter and passes Mary some coins. "This be enough?"

She nods.

"Mind you get a fair price."

She laughs. "And since when 'ave I failed to 'aggle well?"

"Don't be long, we be needing more of the marzipan and biscuits."

"Florence can start on those while I make our dinner." She steps out of the shop.

With the basket over her arm she slowly makes her way towards the market, pausing to share greetings with the many familiar faces along the way. Sunshine warms her soul and she welcomes the opportunity to escape the chores and busyness of the shop. The cobbled streets are bustling with many enjoying the sun and chatting as they go about their business. The heaviness that has been hanging over her lifts. Her heart is glad and her steps light.

A hand touches her elbow. "Mary, 'tis lovely to see you."

"Eleanor, it's been so long. Walk with me a while. Are you 'eading to the market?"

"Of course. 'Ow's Florence and the li'le ones?"

They chat about their families and life in general. Eleanor's husband owns a small bakery business and she bakes the loaves of bread while raising their eight surviving children.

"I've been listening to the men talking about the women's rights movement that started with that Mary Wollstonecraft and 'er book. George is appalled and says it isn't right for women to 'old opinions on politics. 'E says we don't 'ave the intelligence. What you think, Mary?"

Mary shifts the basket to her other arm so she can draw nearer to Eleanor and speaks in a low voice. "I 'eard John tell Edward if women are encouraged to think about such things it would lead to defiance and that would do our men no good at all."

"Bless 'em." Eleanor giggles. "They be right scared; they need us too much for us to be any feistier."

"I find it best to keep the peace and say nought."

"I 'eard George asking John if 'e could imagine what the world would look like if women could vote. 'E said the mere idea was ridiculous and they laughed 'eartily."

"John 'as often said women were created inferior to men and can't expect to understand logic and reason." Mary drops her voice even lower to be sure no one can eavesdrop. "But sometimes I reckon I understand the things them men talk about at least as well as 'e does."

"Best not tell 'em that."

As they enter the market area, a poor woman sits begging. Her hair is matted and grey, her dress in tatters and her face scarred and lined with years of hardship. "'Cuse me lady, got a spare penny?"

Mary pulls out a coin and drops it into her outstretched hand. "Mind you buy bread with it and not the gin."

"Gawd bless ye." Her bloodshot eyes momentarily lock on Mary.

Mary is moved by the poor woman's distress and she wishes there was more she could do to help her.

As they walk away Eleanor places her hand on Mary's arm. "You 'ave a kind soul, Mary, always taking time to care for others."

Mary's arm begins to tremble and she quickly pulls away, not wanting Eleanor to notice. "I pity the woeful women and their nippers in them poor 'ouses. I'm sure it's not always their fault they've been cast a miserable lot. It makes me feel privileged to 'ave me life."

Eleanor hugs her elbow. "You be a good woman, Mary."

As they approach the flower cart Eleanor says, "Mmmm, smell them flowers. Ain't they lovely?"

The colourful cart overflows with an abundance of daffodils, wood anemones, irises, bluebells, cowslips and violets.

"I can't smell 'em," Mary says.

"You can't smell 'em? You must. Their scent is overpowering."

Mary steps across to the cart and bends down to breathe in their scent. "That's strange, I ain't able to smell 'em at all."

"Never mind. Per'aps you're just sickening for something."

The two friends wander on until they are standing outside a grocery shop. Large baskets with a variety of wares adorn the front of the building.

"I must be getting on. John will be wondering what's become of me," Mary says. "But it's been lovely to see you, Eleanor."

"You stay well now. Say 'ello to Florence from me."

They finish their goodbyes with a hug and Mary passes between the baskets to enter the grocer's shop. The interior is gloomy and it takes a minute for her eyes to adjust. Sacks, tubs, boxes and barrels of produce are strewn about the floor and she takes care to step around them. With the purchases made she hastily leaves with the basket heavy over her arm.

6

Rose, Kenya, March 2017

The aisle of the plane is littered with rubbish and discarded airline blankets. Without aircon the atmosphere soon becomes unbearably hot and stuffy. The passengers ahead of me struggle along with their oversized cabin luggage, knocking it against arm rests and seat backs as they hurry to disembark.

As always when travelling on my own I'm filled with a mixture of excited anticipation and trepidation— excited about seeing old friends and embarking on a new adventure, but anxious at being outside my comfort zone, because travelling with Parkinson's is an unknown. My tremor responds with greater intensity, so I take extra care as I negotiate my way down the steep steps to the tarmac where a bus is waiting.

The bus drops us at an airport building. I follow the signs to immigration where I join a queue and listen to the cacophony of voices in different languages that fills the hall. A bored-looking official stamps my passport and waves me through. After collecting my luggage I clear customs and push my trolley through the arrival hall towards the exit. A young man holds a sign with International Needs clearly printed on it. I smile and wave, my built-up tension giving way to excitement as I veer across to him.

Mary and Me

We introduce ourselves and Derek explains we are waiting on others to join us from different flights. He gestures to a vacant seat close by and suggests I wait there. The long flights have taken their toll and I gratefully collapse into it. Although tired, I remain upbeat. The twenty-eight hours in transit between home and Nairobi afforded me time to think and process my diagnosis and uncertain future, leaving me in a better space to face whatever lies ahead.

I'm here for the International Needs congress, my fifth congress as a New Zealand delegate. It's a Christian organisation that is made up of partners from around the globe. Those partners in developing countries identify needs and develop programmes to help meet these needs, while support partners get alongside them and try to provide the resources needed.

"Rose, you're here already." I recognise the lilt in the voice as being Eastern European and turn to see Daniela from Romania drop her bag and spread her arms towards me. It's so good to hug my friend again.

"Daniela, so good to see you, two years is too long. Have you just arrived?"

"Yes, of course. I look forward to these congresses to catch up with you and our friends in the IN family."

"Me too." I stand back and look at this beautiful woman and know that it's a privilege to call her my friend. "I always think of you in Turkey when you stood before us holding up your national flag with a large hole ripped out of it. You gave such a passionate presentation about how the heart has been ripped out of your country. I will never forget."

"But it is so true. We see it with the children."

"You do such amazing work. I would love to visit one day, but that won't be possible."

Daniela's beautiful face breaks into a generous smile. "But you must come."

"I think this will be my last overseas trip." I can hear the emotion in my own voice.

"No, why?"

"Long story. I don't want to bore you with it now, not when you've just arrived."

Her face crumples into a frown as her large, dark eyes search mine. "Please tell me, what's wrong?"

"I've just found out I have Parkinson's disease. It's a degenerative illness."

"I know it," she says. "That's terrible."

"I'm still coming to terms with it. And we don't know what my future will hold, how long I can stay healthy. I'm retiring from my work including my IN responsibilities." My voice trembles as I add, "I've really come to say goodbye."

Her eyes widen and she moves to hug me again. "So sorry."

Her genuine concern causes me to tear up and I fight to keep it together, my emotions barely below the surface after the long-haul flights. I change the subject and we begin to exchange flight experiences.

"Hola, Rose, Daniela!" José approaches us wheeling a large bag, his camera swinging side to side around his neck as he struggles under the cabin luggage hanging over his shoulder.

Mary and Me

"Hola, mi amigo." This is about the extent of my Spanish and I grin sheepishly. "Good to see you."

He nods at me, grinning broadly, but I know his English is about as good as my Spanish. It's very cool how you can become friends without a common language.

Others join us, both old and new acquaintances, and we wait in a small yet noisy huddle for our minivan. We are Kiwi, Romanian, Columbian, Ethiopian, Zambian and a Brit. The excitement is infectious and I soon forget my jet lag.

Our destination is Brackenhurst, a couple of hours from the airport. Derek provides a travel commentary as we skirt around Nairobi and out to the countryside; past the airport hotels and buildings, past open spaces where he says he saw a zebra earlier, past markets, past slum areas, past leafy green plantations, before finally turning into a side road. There's a stream on the left where people are washing. The van labours as it climbs a hill and pulls into a driveway, coming to rest in front of a reception office.

We climb out and I take in my surroundings. A majestic, colonial style, white-washed building is its centre piece. Its steep red roof has an attic window and a tall chimney. Wide steps lead up to the main entrance on the second floor and its black timber gives it a Tudor-like feel. Arched windows feature on the lower floor and large rectangular windows, divided into a myriad of small panes, dominate the second floor. Smaller outbuildings, also white-washed with red roofs, are dotted around the expansive grounds, separated by manicured green lawn and mature trees.

"Wow, this place is awesome." I take my bag from Derek.

His teeth gleam white against his skin as he grins with pride. "Thank you. It was used by the British as a military hospital during World War 1 and is now a conference centre. We have about forty hectares of grounds."

I check in and am shown the way to my room. Once freshened up I take a wander about the immediate vicinity to get my bearings. Although it's been 31 hours since leaving home I'm feeling surprisingly upbeat after reconnecting with old friends and the gentle exercise calms the quivering in my muscles.

My fear about how my Parkinson's would react to the travel was unfounded. I managed the timing for the pills as we flew across time zones by simply dividing my normal three-times-a-day dose into eight-hour intervals. As a result, I hope to drop straight into the Kenyan time zone, even though it is nine hours behind New Zealand. My body seems to have adjusted and my tremor hasn't caused me any more issues than it does at home. Even my Parkinson's bladder hadn't caused a problem. When it decides it's time to go, there's often not a lot of warning. Thankfully, my bookings were all for aisle seats.

Now safe among friends I can relax and enjoy their company.

*

The time goes by far too quickly. Our delegates number about 45 and when we're not in meetings our time is spent catching up with each other. The days are exhausting and I'm buzzing with the old vitality, more so than I've felt in a long time. I'm open about my recent diagnosis and it's no secret that this is likely to be my last congress.

I advise my colleagues of my intention to pull out of my committees.

We enjoy a Kenyan-style barbecue and cultural evening, being entertained with a variety of African dances from different tribal groups performed by talented dancers in traditional costumes. It's hilarious to watch some of the non-African visitors try out their African dance moves, especially in the fertility dance. I stand back and take photos, no longer confident to join in as I once would have.

The next day we board a bus and are taken out to visit some of the projects run by our partner in Kenya. Education in Kenya is a privilege and not a right. It's only thanks to the generosity of foreign sponsors that many of these children get to go to school.

The coach navigates a maze of alleyways, turning red dirt into clouds of dust in our wake, before we pull up on the outskirts of Kawangware, one of Nairobi's slums. We leave our bags on the bus and step outside into the hot sunshine.

"We have a project here working with the street children," Jocelyn, Executive Director of International Needs Kenya, says. "Follow me and we'll visit some of the enterprises."

The road is lined with a series of corrugated iron sheds and lean-tos, their rust matching the dirt of the road. Men stop their work and openly stare, reminding me how much of an oddity we must look—a coachload of people of varying skin colours and ethnicities.

Across the road is a tin shed where some youths are waiting. Inside the shed a workshop is fitted out with a range of tools and furniture. Stephen was once a street kid who now owns his own business making furniture as a result of the programme. It's a tribute to the success of the programme that he now employs other street kids and is teaching them carpentry skills. Our visit is short, for as long as we foreigners linger in front of his workshop the customers stay away.

Jocelyn leads us to a car washing place where she introduces us to the team of street kids working there. Living on the street for these kids means a constant battle with alcohol and drug addictions as well as rape.

I approach one of the women, named Clara, whose face is pocked with acne and scars, her hair in dreads.

"Hi Clara, how long have you worked in this business?" I ask.

"Six years," she says. "Since my baby was born."

"You have a six-year-old?" I smile. "You look too young."

"I have three children," Clara answers. "They are eighteen, sixteen and six. I was ten when I had my first baby."

Stunned, I wonder if I misunderstood her accent. "Ten years old?"

"Yes, ten," she repeats. "I raised my children on the street."

I try to fathom how a ten-year-old child can have a baby and live on the street, when ten-year-olds should be innocent and playing with dolls. "What has the project done for you?" I ask.

"I had a drug addiction, but now I'm drug free for the project. The money I get working in the car wash helps

Mary and Me

me to feed my family." Clara smiles and her face lights up. "The project has just given me a hairdressing apprenticeship. That's what I really want to do. I start next week."

"That's wonderful. Congratulations!" I am genuinely pleased for her. "What's your dream? If you could choose anything at all, what would you want most?"

Clara's dark, brown eyes fix on mine. "To change a life, just as mine has been changed by the project."

She could've said to own a flash car or a house or countless other material things, but this is a real transformation—to pay forward what she has received.

Jocelyn rounds us up and we head for the bus. As we struggle along I see a sign with a picture of Nelson Mandela, his face lit with a smile. It reads *The greatest glory in living lies not in never falling, but in rising every time we fall.*

Next stop is Kibera, the largest slum in Africa and one of the most densely populated places on the planet. Jocelyn fills us in on the horror story that is Kibera. Life expectancy here is thirty years of age and half the population are aged under fifteen. One out of five children don't make their fifth birthday. The shacks are without running water and one million people share six hundred toilets. Girls are routinely raped and HIV is rife. The comparison to my own life is incomprehensible.

"We are concerned for your safety inside Kibera so we have arranged for bodyguards to guide you through and the bus will pick us up at the other side." Jocelyn looks nervous under the weight of responsibility of keeping her guests safe. "Please leave your cameras on the bus because they'll attract too much attention. If you want a photo, just ask one of the bodyguards to take it for you on a mobile phone."

We leave the cool interior and step out into the dry heat. The land slopes away from the road and a sea of rusty corrugated-iron roofs fills the landscape. We make for a corrugated iron building the size of a barn in a compound with an iron fence and are ushered inside where green plastic chairs are laid out on a dirt floor. The heat inside is suffocating as we listen to the youth leaders talk about the amazing projects underway with the youth in Kibera. Light dazzles like stars through the multitude of nail holes in the iron walls.

We walk through a labyrinth of shacks and lean-tos, where entire families share a single room the size of my ensuite. Some have brightly-coloured curtains over the entrances, others are just a hole in the wall with no obvious door for protection.

A woman watches us from a doorway; her dark face lined and gaunt, her clothes in tatters and the brightly-coloured fabric, so typical in Africa, is faded with filth. What draws me to her are the tremors that so obviously shake her body.

Coming alongside one of our Kenyan hosts, I ask, "Stephen, are there many cases of Parkinson's disease in Kenya?"

"I honestly don't know. There's a lot of stigma surrounding the disease and we have many people thinking it's caused by witchcraft, especially in remote rural areas. So it's likely people just choose to hide their condition. Unfortunately, superstition breeds fear."

"Are there any treatments available?"

"Of course, but mostly in the cities. In many of the rural areas and slums the people are left undiagnosed and untreated. It would be difficult to know how many actually suffer from it if they don't go to medical clinics."

Living under a shroud of superstition is a huge obstacle in so many cultures and once more I say a quick prayer, thankful for the country and the time I live in.

We pick our way cautiously along red and dusty paths, stepping over and around the sewerage and rubbish. The smell is intensified by the prickly heat. Curious eyes follow our progress through this pit of human poverty—perhaps resentful towards wealthy foreigners who come for ghetto tourism.

A toddler sits on the dirt in front of a mud hut, her large white eyes watching. Mud and rock fill the stick structure, forming solid walls. The doorway is missing a door and the interior is void of furniture. A single cooking pot sits on the dirt floor.

"Hello," she says in clear English. Her hair is braided with brightly-coloured beads and her beautiful round young face shines with the innocence of a child. She's dressed in a bright pink top with white leggings, not unlike any child anywhere in the world.

"Hello, what's your name?" asks Esther, the Nepalese delegate.

"Lucy." She beams her pretty smile.

What sort of resilience and human grit does it take to survive Kibera, especially if you are a girl? I can only pray that she is one of the children who'll receive hope through the project work of Jocelyn and her staff who dedicate their lives to helping the poorest of the poor.

The visits leave me feeling very privileged and I realise that dealing with Parkinson's is nothing compared to the struggles so many in this world cope with.

*

I get up early and hurriedly splash water on my face to chase the tiredness away before changing into shorts, T-shirt and sneakers. Today is the last day of the congress and I've been awake since the early hours, revisiting the kaleidoscope of meetings and experiences since leaving New Zealand last week.

I open the door to another beautiful day in this piece of Kenyan paradise and immediately my spirits lift. Danny, one of the delegates, is already waiting at our meeting place.

"Hi, ready for another walk?" he asks.

"Sure am. Do you want to go down the road to the place where the locals do their washing?" I ask.

"That sounds like a decent walk."

"I've really appreciated you walking with me, as I probably wouldn't have been brave enough to go walking outside the estate on my own."

We walk in silence as we head for the security gate at the entrance to the property. The security guard greets us as he opens the gate to let us through and we turn to walk along the edge of the road.

"I'm sorry if I'm not good company this morning. I didn't sleep well and I'm sad to think this is probably my last-ever congress and maybe even my last international trip," I say.

"Why do you think that?"

"We don't know how fast my symptoms will develop, so there're no guarantees."

Mary and Me

Danny is silent, so I carry on. "I came here intending to step down from my responsibilities and to say goodbye. But it's not so easy. I love this work and there are so few volunteers who have the time to work on the governance committees."

"Why do you think you should give it up if you are still loving the work and have the ability to do it?"

"Good question. To be really honest, I worry about my cognitive function. I've lost confidence and feel I'm not as sharp as I used to be. My attention span and multi-tasking ability seems worse and I forget words more than I used to. I'm especially hopeless with names."

"I've not noticed. Are you sure?"

"I think so, although Gary says he can't see any evidence of it and it's probably just a natural ageing thing that most people get. However, I know what goes on in my head and sometimes I feel like I'm spinning, looking for the right words. I don't want to be on committees if I can't give 100 per cent."

"What are you going to do about the new strategic advisory group then?"

"I've tried to turn it down but I'm being talked into it. After all it's only for two years." I laugh. "I came here with the intention of standing down from two committees and I'm leaving with my name attached to three. The work tends to get into the blood and it's hard to say no."

"That's a good thing. We need the volunteers who are passionate and prepared to put the time in. Look, for what it's worth, I think you should continue with the work you love until such time you really feel you can't do it any longer. Don't let fear take that away from you. You don't want to sell yourself short and give in to your disease prematurely."

"Thanks." We walk in silence as I ponder his words. *Danny is right, I can't let fear get in the way and right now I seem to be coping.*

The road is lined with trees and shrubs, their shades of green in stark contrast to the orange-red soil of a track meandering alongside the road. The road winds down a steep slope and at the bottom is the dam I'd noticed on our arrival. Upstream the water is perfectly still in the early morning, reflecting the image of the opposite bank. Locals with buckets of washing congregate in small groups at the water's edge, carrying out their chores before going to their places of work. Snatches of their sing-song voices and laughter carry across the still water.

It's a fascinating picture of community that is missing in the west. I turn my camera on, zoom in and check the settings—high ISO so I can use a fast shutter speed to get around the tremor—and snap the shot. Despite living in a culture where this strong community spirit has been lost I'm filled with gratitude. Thankful to be born into my family in New Zealand at this time in history, thankful to have an automatic washing machine and all the modern conveniences, thankful for my life, with or without Parkinson's.

*

Today's lunch comes at the end of the formal meetings and the delegates are buzzing. The week has been long and productive with significant progress made on several fronts. The delegates are united in their passion to see the

Mary and Me

organisation grow in strength. It's a social occasion, with limited time left before we go our separate ways once more.

Santosh approaches, his smile lighting up his eyes. "Can I join you?" he asks, indicating the empty chair.

"Of course."

He puts his plate of mixed meats and vegetables on the table and sits beside me. I have huge respect for this gentle Indian man who has led our congress over the last few years. His disc jockey past is reflected in his blue-rimmed glasses, the perfect accompaniment to his goatee, which now has more salt than pepper.

"How have you found the congress this year?" he asks.

"It's been great, one of the best yet. I think we've made some good progress. Thanks for all your hard work."

"When does Gary get here?"

"Tomorrow. I'm to meet him at Nairobi airport and I can't wait. We're overnighting in Nairobi then flying out to the Maasai Mara for a safari before holidaying in Uganda. We've decided to make the most of my being here and take the opportunity to have the holiday of a lifetime. I always wanted to go on a safari."

"Sounds wonderful." Santosh looks thoughtful as he takes a forkful of food. "We've asked Peter to lead us in a healing service this afternoon as part of our closing ceremony. I wanted to ask if you would be happy for us to pray specifically for you during the service?"

Peter is a Kenyan pastor who leads one of the youth projects. He impressed me as a man of deep faith and quiet humility, eager to know how you and your family are and quick to probe your needs, for him to commit them to prayer.

"Yes, that would be special." As the significance of this gesture sinks in, I add, "I would be honoured, thank you."

"Peter will probably call you to the front of the room. Is that okay with you?"

"Yes, of course." My faith is an important part of who I am. I believe my strength comes from the hope I have in Jesus Christ and in my salvation through him.

We are soon joined by others and I excuse myself to go out and take some photos of the centre.

*

Peter stands at the front of the conference room. He has changed out of his casual western clothes and is wearing the traditional black garb and collar of the Anglican church. This gentle and humble Kenyan man is of slight build and yet when he speaks his voice resonates with a firm assurance that commands attention.

The service begins with a time of thanksgiving. Fifty strong voices blend together to fill the room with song. It has a deep, rich harmony, creating something that is moving and beautiful. Peter then calls me to the front and asks if the other delegates would like to come and stand with me. As they pray for my healing I'm overwhelmed with God's love for me and with the love of these national leaders whom I'm privileged to call my friends. Tears flow freely and I allow them to run down my cheeks unchecked, as if washing the disease away. There is no instant healing, but something changes inside me.

A picture of the paralytic man comes to mind, the one who went to Jesus to ask for healing. Jesus said, "Get up. Pick up your mat and walk."

It's time to get up and do my bit to fight this Parkinson's. It's time to pick up my mat and to start walking.

Through faith I have the confidence that comes with knowing that everything will be okay, and it's this reassurance that will help me face my uncertain future.

The remainder of the day is spent saying goodbyes to my friends. This work has been a big part of my life and when the time comes for me to be released from my duties, I will miss it, but not nearly as much as I will miss this unique international family.

7

Rose, Kenya, March 2017

I stare out the window of the plane at the huge expanse of green pasture below, dotted with bushy trees and totally devoid of fences for as far as the eye can see. The ground slowly comes up to meet us and I can see an air strip with a few safari vehicles waiting by a small shed.

"Look, elephants!" I nudge Gary in the ribs.

The pilot opens the throttle and the plane responds, gaining speed and altitude before we begin to circle the air strip.

"Just going around again to give the elephants time to move away from the landing strip." The speaker crackles with static and the voice battles the whine of the engine.

Startled by the plane the elephants slowly move away, allowing us to touch down and taxi to the shed. The pilot opens the door and we are hit by a wave of heat.

"Welcome to the Maasai Mara," he says.

We duck through the small opening and down the steps.

Gary looks at me grinning, "Let the safari begin!"

A man called Ben collects us and our luggage. As we pile into an open-sided, open-topped jeep he tells us he is Maasai and he'll be our driver-cum-guide.

The red dirt track stretches out ahead of us and we bounce from pothole to pothole. A family of giraffes stand on the track blocking our path and watch our progress with mild curiosity. Ben slows to a stop. A young giraffe, its head no higher than the adult's back, cranes its neck around to see what is making the disturbance.

"Look!" I grab my camera.

Ben laughs. "You'll see plenty of those while you're here. You can stand up if you want. You'll get a better view looking out over the roof. And let me know if you want to stop for photos."

We stand leaning on the frame of the jeep and look around. More goofy-looking giraffes pop their heads up above the bushes they are chewing on, momentarily distracted by the arrival of our jeep.

My camera works overtime.

"You have picked a good time to visit," Ben says. "It is springtime and there are baby animals everywhere. Also, the grass isn't so high now that you can't spot the animals, but it provides enough good food for the grazers. Neither are there many tourists about because it is the start of the rainy season. The pattern is for it to rain overnight, leaving the days clear."

"That's just perfect," I say. I turn to Gary and add, "Lucky congress was at the right time."

"I expect some awesome photos," he says.

We arrive at the Mara Serena safari lodge and check into our rooms. We're warned not to leave our balcony door open as baboons could come in and steal our things. The lodge is on a small hill overlooking the Mara and from our balcony I can see herds of giraffe, zebra, elephants and antelopes in the distance.

We are scheduled to have a safari drive each morning and evening during our three-day stay, as that is when the animals are at their most active. That leaves us to relax at the resort during the heat of the day when they are resting.

After a leisurely lunch we explore our surroundings before heading to the pool for the afternoon. We've lots to catch up on. The weeks following my diagnosis have been challenging, with Gary's slow internal processor at odds with my rapid external processor, creating a small amount of unease between us.

"You seem happy and relaxed," Gary says from the lounger next to mine. Water glistens in the sunlight as it drips from his tanned body.

"I feel so energised." I take the hand he offers. "It's so exciting. I can hardly wait for the safari. I really want to see lions, cheetahs and leopards."

"Patience, Grasshopper," he says. It's an old joke, but we laugh anyway.

A movement catches my eye—a brightly-coloured red, blue and grey lizard perched on the dry, stone wall adjacent to our loungers shifts lazily while soaking up the hot afternoon sun.

"Look." I pick up my camera. "He's so stunning, too perfect to be made by chance."

"Sure is."

We are silent for a while.

"There is life after a Parkinson's diagnosis and it can be a good life," I muse.

Mary and Me

"We should never doubt it. To do so only puts limitations on us."

"You're so very right. I was expecting to find the travel this time around too hard, too exhausting. I really believed this would be my last overseas trip, but I'm handling it and Parkinson's can't take this away. My symptoms are no worse. In fact, I feel great."

"I was also worried this may be our last trip and I was determined to make the most of it. And I was worried about you travelling on your own and how your body would cope with the stress of it. I'm relieved to see you looking so much better—less stressed, I think."

"Yeah, I think I am less stressed. In fact, I feel less apathetic and more determined to fight. In a way, it's like I've picked up my mat and have started walking, walking towards improved well-being, if not a cure."

"That's my girl." Gary squeezes my hand. "How about we use the gym while we're here? It can be the start of getting serious about fighting."

"Maybe tomorrow morning after breakfast?"

"Deal. And when we return home you should get serious about your research, treat it like a client's project." He pauses, before adding, "The more you know about the enemy you're facing the more successful your fight will be."

We lapse into silence, both lost in our own thoughts. Above me, a yellow weaver bird works on its nest that hangs from a palm frond.

I know Gary's right. After all, I've fought and overcome adversity before. I learned then it's how I respond to it that's important. That's what I have control over. I need to focus on the positives, even though there aren't too many. But neither were there many positives when I was attacked and strangled, yet I managed to find some. I prided myself on my ability to stay positive then and I can do it again.

Parkinson's does not—no, a correction—will not define me. I am not Parkinson's, no more than I am flu when I have influenza. My body merely hosts it. Up until now a silent giant has been stealing my brain cells, but with the diagnosis I can prepare to do battle. The research can start as soon as I'm home.

"I need to learn as much as I can about Parkinson's and fight it on all possible fronts," I say aloud, although really musing to myself. "I've only just realised that I've been living with fear, fear of the future and its uncertainty. And fear can be paralysing, a downward spiral. It's time I stand against it and fight."

"I like the sound of that." He looks at me, his eyes wide and glistening.

"It's hard. The symptoms never stop and they're a constant reminder. It can be all-consuming, but somehow I need to rise above it."

"One of the things I love about you is your courage. We'll fight this together, one day at a time."

I reach out for his hand. "I'm so thankful for you."

He gives my hand a gentle squeeze. "C'mon, enough sop. Let's go and get ready for the safari."

We pick up our things and carry them back to our room.

*

We are joined in the jeep by a young Indian couple on their honeymoon, Maneesh and Prisha. The four of us

Mary and Me

stand in the four corners of the jeep as Ben drives us down the red dirt track. It is late afternoon and I can barely contain my excitement. My camera is set and ready, mounted on its monopod with the foot on the floor of the jeep. I clench it tightly in my good hand to prevent it hitting the metal bar as we bump across the savannah.

First stop is the river, where twenty to thirty hippos of all sizes congregate in the deep water. Their cute little round ears, bulging eyes and nostrils peek above the surface of the water and belie the hulk that is submerged, not unlike an iceberg. My shutter clicks. Two hippos sense our presence and put on a play fight, as if for our entertainment. More clicks.

"Hippos are herbivores and graze at night when it is cool. During the day they wallow in the water to keep their skin cool and moist and to protect it from the sun." Ben points to the nearest edge. "Do you see that?"

It is a very large crocodile, possibly the biggest I've ever seen. My skin tingles as I imagine having to get out of the jeep into its territory. I shudder. A rock moves and I realise it's not just one crocodile, as many of the other rocks are also partially submerged crocs. My shutter clicks some more.

"Do you carry a gun?" Gary asks.

"No gun," Ben answers. "If we did, the only thing we'd shoot would be the poachers."

"What about a tranquiliser gun?" Maneesh asks.

"No tranquiliser. The animals in the park are used to humans in vehicles. They don't pose a threat. Only the male elephants get threatening at times and we get out of their way."

Ben kicks the jeep into life and we head back up onto the track. Looking out across the plains that are rich in wildlife he identifies hairless hartebeests with their notched and crooked horns, water bucks covered in furry coats, graceful impala, and the black and tan hairless topi.

In the late afternoon light a strong and impressive topi stands silently on one of the mounds of earth scattered across the vast plains. Antelopes of all types graze around him. Ben explains a topi will often stand guard on the anthills to warn others of impending danger. My camera captures the moment.

We stop as a herd of elephants cross our tracks. They are close, very close. They eye us with unmasked curiosity. A baby elephant having a dirt bath loosens the dirt with its foot, picks it up in its trunk and throws it over its back. One of the larger elephants calls out and the baby trots over to her. The baby's mother then walks onto the road only metres in front of our jeep and stops. Watching us she relieves herself and copious quantities of steaming liquid hit the dry dirt and splash widely. Then she ambles away, baby in tow. I'm in my happy place, snapping photos to transform the experience into lasting memories.

We follow the red dirt road further across the plains, slowing as a pair of ostriches, their feathery coats quivering, run towards us and cross in front of our jeep.

The road winds down into a shallow valley where herds of zebra, water buffalo and giraffe graze together. Ben brakes to a stop.

"Do you see the jittery way the herd moves?" he asks, pointing to the zebras. "There'll be a pride of lions about. If we're lucky you might see them."

We scan the area seeing only the grazing animals. I zoom in on a fat zebra and take an image of mesmerising black and white stripes, perhaps designed as a clever defence mechanism to confuse predators.

As if Ben hears my thoughts he says, "The zebra stripes are unique to each animal, like fingerprints. They provide camouflage and help to protect them from the biting insects. Did you know lions are colour blind?"

"No, that's interesting," answers Gary, who stands closest to Ben.

"We often find giraffes grazing with the zebras. With their height they can see the predators first and will warn the other animals." Ben switches off the motor. "We'll just wait here and see if we can spot the lions."

Behind me, Maneesh and Prisha make approving remarks about our guide.

We wait. I play with making different compositions of the giraffes and zebras, happy in my role as photographer. The light is becoming infused with gold as twilight approaches.

"How large is the Mara?" Gary asks.

"1,510 square kilometres," our guide replies. "But it's more than that for the animals. It joins the Serengeti, the largest park in Tanzania, without fences. The Serengeti is 14,750 square kilometres. The animals don't recognise borders and roam freely across the two parks."

"Wow, that's massive."

"Look!" Ben points.

We follow his outstretched finger and see a movement in the grass. Ben starts the engine and slowly moves closer, then stops again.

A lioness stands and looks our way, perhaps to see the source of the disturbance. Beside her another lioness lies on her side. Further movement reveals cubs tumbling in the grass.

"Look—cubs. And she's feeding them." My camera goes crazy as I try to capture the scene before it disappears.

"How many can you see?" Maneesh asks.

"Six, maybe eight?"

A cub nips playfully at the lioness and she swats it away. It walks around her, rubbing up against her like a kitten. But this is no kitten; it's a wild lion. I watch in wonderment, scarcely able to believe what I am seeing. Such a privilege to see these big cats with their cubs in the wild.

A lioness gets up and walks away. I notice two older cubs playing twenty metres from her and she moves towards them in slow strong strides. The cubs look up and scamper towards her. She pauses to look in our direction and turns to meander towards us. Closer and closer she comes until she's just metres from our jeep. So close now, I can see her yellowy-green eyes. Beside me Gary stiffens. We are quiet, holding our collective breath. The silence is only broken by the sound of my camera as it works furiously to document the scene.

Walking around our jeep the lioness puts us between her and her cubs. She scowls, showing two menacing yellow incisors before flopping down on the dirt. Her pink tongue licks her black liquorice-coloured lips. Flies buzz about her and she twitches her scarred face in annoyance. The cubs are playing on the dirt track, still on the opposite side of our vehicle, oblivious they are putting us in danger. The lioness stands, stretches lazily then walks away back towards the second lioness who is still feeding her cubs. The two cubs follow, the seed heads of the grass parting to let them through.

The light is fading fast now as we bump our way back. Gary asks, "How did you feel about that?"

"Wow, words can't describe it. It's hard to believe we've seen lions in the wild and so close. It was simply amazing."

"Were you scared?" His voice lowers, barely audible over the noise of the jeep.

"I was too busy taking photos and it didn't cross my mind. I reckon I've got some really good shots."

"I admit I was a bit scared. She's a wild animal and it would be nothing for her to drag one of us out the side of the jeep. It was a bit too close for my liking, especially with no tranquiliser gun on board."

I look at his earnest face. "I didn't even think about that."

"It was a bit sobering and yet incredible. Talk about 'seize the day'."

By the time we park outside the resort it is already dark. The honeymoon couple invite us to join them for dinner. We cover the usual small talk and discover Maneesh works for a construction company in Egypt and Prisha has resigned from her career as a software developer in Bengaluru to join him. They glow with the radiance of newlyweds.

"I hope you don't mind me saying that I've noticed you have a tremor," says Maneesh. "My dad has one. He was diagnosed with Parkinson's disease twelve years ago."

"Was he? Sorry to hear that. I've been diagnosed with it too. Is there much Parkinson's in India?" I ask.

"I honestly can't say. Do you watch TED Talks?" Maneesh asks.

"Just the occasional ones—generally only if I come across one being shared on Facebook."

"There's one you might be interested in, on Parkinson's. My dad found it inspirational. Can I show you?" Maneesh fiddles with his phone, then passes it to me.

Gary and I put our heads together as we watch. A young attractive Indian woman in western dress fills the small screen. She tells how she set out to improve the quality of life for her favourite uncle who has Parkinson's. First, she noticed that he had difficulties drinking from a cup without spilling, so she invented one with curved sides that force any potential spillages to slosh back into the cup and not over the sides. She then shows a clip of her uncle walking with a walker. He has bradykinesia and walks slowly, dragging his feet. She says she found that when he walks up or down stairs his gait becomes normal and he has no need for any support, but when on the flat he can no longer walk without the support of his walker. She then shows how she photographed some stairs and printed them on a large scale and laid them on the floor like a mat, from his bed to the bathroom and then to the living area. Her uncle then walks on the photograph of the stairs and it's obvious his movements are fluid and he doesn't need any assistance. Then, as soon as he goes to move off the mat he freezes and needs his walker.

"Wow." I'm genuinely impressed. "That's so fascinating."

"My dad says he's using different parts of the brain. The automatic movements are controlled by the part that's damaged, but when he comes to stairs his brain switches to control the movements deliberately."

"Perhaps the trick would be to harness that for everyday movements," Gary adds.

"It's certainly reason for hope. The brain's so complex and it seems we understand so little of how it works. I did hear of a person in a rest home with advanced Parkinson's who, when someone called *fire*, leapt out of bed to run outside. It sounds bizarre, but Parkinson's is a very strange illness." I pause to look at Maneesh. "How's your dad doing?"

"Not so good. He is struggling to walk and has a lot of falls."

"I'm sorry to hear that." Emotion threatens my outer calm and I change the topic to safer ground. "Tell us about your wedding."

We chat about their elaborate Indian wedding and Prisha shows us some photos. She and Maneesh made a beautiful and very regal-looking bridal couple in their red and ivory wedding outfits complete with head gear.

Back in our room we get ready for bed, exhausted from our day's adventures.

We haven't been in bed long when a flash of light fills our small room, followed by a clap of thunder. More lightning and thunder follow, the seconds between them decrease as the storm approaches. The rain is heavy on the roof and the balcony furniture.

"Let's watch the lightning over the plains." I get out of bed to pull the curtain aside. Something large and black moves on the other side of the glass. I yelp as it bares its teeth and hisses at me. A baboon is taking shelter on our balcony and we laugh at the absurdity of it.

"I'm not sure who just got the biggest fright, you or him."

I watch the lightning zig and zag across the sky. "I guess that might be it for the safari. It might be too wet tomorrow."

"We'll just have to go with the flow."

We return to bed and I eventually fall asleep, hoping today's adventure won't be the last of the safari drives.

The alarm whirs and I'm immediately awake. It is dark and quiet outside. I look through the curtains and the star-studded night sky lifts my spirits as I realise that the storm has passed.

Ben, already waiting in our jeep, tells us that one of the rangers has phoned to say there is a fresh lion kill somewhere in the park. He drives at pace and I hold on tight as we bump along the potholes. It is just the three of us as the honeymooners are taking a hot air balloon ride.

As the sun rises over the savannah we observe a hippo ambling slowly to its waterhole after a long night of grazing.

We slow down and quietly approach the area of the kill. The remains of a zebra, its black and white stripes covered in blood, lies beneath two lionesses who are pulling flesh from the carcass and devouring it greedily. Half a dozen other lionesses are scattered among the long grass, their bellies distended from feasting. Off to the side sits the pride's male, his mane majestic as he watches over his harem. A dozen hyenas wait in a semicircle around the

Mary and Me

pride, only their heads with their trademark round ears visible above the long grass—no doubt drooling while they wait their turn. But the lions aren't finished yet. The male stands slowly and wanders across to the feast to have his share, or perhaps it's dessert. The feast is a photographer's dream and I give my camera a good workout.

A lone hyena with a torn ear stands on the track, its dark eyes appearing to show evil intent. Its coat is spotty and its sturdy legs bowed.

"Most people think the hyena is a dog, but it's not," Ben informs us. "Although closer to the cat family, they are neither cat nor dog."

"It's so ugly." I take its photo.

I look back as the feast continues. Life in the wild really is the survival of the fittest. For many it's a constant fight to have enough food and to not become food themselves. Each day has its own struggles and these animals can live only one day at a time. Perhaps it's not so different for us. I can learn from this and fight my Parkinson's one day at a time. To be the best I can be, the most well I can be, and to enjoy each day with whatever blessings and challenges it brings.

Having seen enough of them gorging we continue along the track in search of leopards, only to encounter a family of warthogs, with the sow suckling its young. Hairier than pigs, the adults have a mane along their spine. Two adults cross our path, their hooves giving them the appearance of wearing stiletto heels. I chuckle.

Ahead, two jeeps are stationary on the track and we pull up behind them for another great photo opportunity. Two huge black rhinos, their cumbersome bodies swaying, trot towards us. Their horns, mounted on misshapen heads with hooked lips, appear sharp and ominous. God must have had a good laugh when he created these creatures.

"You are very lucky," Ben says. "There are only ten rhinos remaining in the Mara and you're seeing two of them."

"Why so few?" Gary asks.

"Poachers. It's been very bad. There's money in their horns. There used to be about 120 black rhino here, but they were often left for dead with their heads bloody from the hacking off of their horns. It's an illegal trade, yet that doesn't seem to stop them."

"Where's the market?"

"Mainly the black market in China and Vietnam, where rhino horn is often ground to a powder and ingested as a treatment for everything from cancer to sea snake bites and hangovers."

"Such a crime."

"Do you know why it's called black rhino?" Ben asks.

"Are some black?"

"No, they are grey or brown, similar to the white rhino. It's said the white rhino was a misinterpretation of the Afrikaans word for 'wide', as they have a square jaw. So then, the hook-lipped ones were called black."

The rhinos saunter across the road between the two front vehicles, unaware of the treasure they wear on their snouts. A bit too close for my comfort.

As we continue our journey our attention is drawn to a herd of elephants stampeding.

"Ben, is there a lion around causing them to stampede?" I ask.

"No. Three years ago a baby elephant was killed near here by a poacher. It's true that elephants don't forget and now these elephants stampede whenever they see a jeep approach."

The elephants run into a grove of bushy trees. As we near, a large male comes out and faces us, grinding its foot into the dust and looking menacing. Ben stops and begins to reverse up the track. Thankfully, the large leathery beast is only threatening and allows us to get out of its territory.

When we near the border with Tanzania we see a pair of spotted cheetahs basking in the early morning sun. Sensing our presence they stand and flex their strong rangy bodies.

"Cheetahs are the fastest land animal. They can sprint at over 110 kilometres per hour," Ben says.

Gary turns to me. "Now that is impressive."

"See that concrete block over there?" Ben points to a single concrete marker standing about waist height. "That's the border with Tanzania. On the other side of that block is the Serengeti."

He drives closer and we stop and get out to stand on Tanzanian ground for the obligatory photo. It's a nervous moment as I consider what might be hiding in the long grass.

On the way home we get to see the elusive leopard, draped over a limb high up in a tree.

"You're good, Ben. I would never have spotted that," Gary says.

"You're lucky with this one too. Many people don't get to see the leopards." Ben stops the jeep.

I line up the leopard in the frame and take the photo. Then, as if on cue, it stands and makes its way along the branch to the trunk and down the tree, disappearing into the undergrowth.

We are almost back at the resort when Ben turns on to a narrow potholed track that takes us into some low bush.

He stops in a clearing and switches the engine off. "Now for your treat. This morning the local Maasai are hosting your breakfast beside the hippos and crocodiles."

I look at Gary in alarm, but he smiles back reassuringly. "They wouldn't do it if they thought it wasn't safe," he murmurs, knowing what is on my mind.

Ben leads us through the bush to a clearing where a Maasai warrior stands, tall and proud, leaning on a wooden stick. He is dressed in the traditional red blanket, draped and tied like a cape, over a blue-and-red tartan cloth wrapped around his slender frame. Layers of colourful and intricate beads decorate his neck, his shaven head adorned with a few thin beaded braids pulled around and tied on his forehead.

Ben introduces him. "This is Moses and he'll be your host this morning."

Moses is standing in front of a table with glasses and champagne bottles and we introduce ourselves as he hands us a glass of bubbles.

With a glass of the delicious golden bubbly in hand we follow him further into the bush alongside the river and past tables scattered through the bush at discreet distances from one another, presumably for other tourists. The tables are set with a white linen cloth and napkins, white china and silverware. The seats are completely covered in the red check fabric of the Maasai. A ranger, gun over his shoulder, is barely visible through the bush, presumably patrolling the area to ensure the visitors are safe from the crocs and any other wildlife that might happen upon the strange gathering.

Moses takes us to a table on the riverbank adjacent to a deep hole where at least twenty hippos are submerged. The bank is about one metre above the river and a couple of crocs are on the sandy edge of the water. My hand and leg instantly shake more violently as I acknowledge their close proximity.

"Is this safe?" I can't help but ask the obvious question of Moses.

Moses grins, his white, even teeth prominent against his dark skin making his face shine even more. "Yes, of course." His voice is deep and rhythmic. "The bank here is too high for the crocodiles to climb up."

I want to believe him, reassured that a croc attack won't do their tourism chances any good and so it must be safe, but my tremor suggests otherwise. I sip my champagne to calm my tremor down and feel its effect almost immediately.

"Come," Moses says. "I will show you the buffet."

He leads us through the bush away from the river to another clearing where long tables covered in white linen display a veritable smorgasbord of delicious food.

"Wow, Moses we were not expecting this." I look around at the lavish setting. "It looks absolutely amazing. Thank you."

"It is our pleasure. It is part of the package deal with your resort." His English is perfect.

"Where do we start?" It's been a long morning already and I know Gary will be starving.

We help ourselves to bacon, sausages, eggs, tomatoes, mushrooms and potatoes, followed by fresh fruit. The food smells and looks good. We soak in the surroundings as we eat. Champagne is the perfect accompaniment to a very surreal experience.

After breakfast Moses walks us back towards the jeep.

"How important is tourism to your village?" Gary asks.

"Very. We need it to finance our way of life. I would not have been able to go away to school without the tourism."

"Do you think it's changing your culture?" I ask.

"Not really. Maasai are a proud people and we love our culture. We hold on to it with strong hands. Many of our young people go away to school and university, but we are expected to come back. Of course not everyone does and there is a drift into the cities for work and the lifestyle."

We return to the resort, satiated and thankful for this extraordinary experience.

Once back in our room Gary and I go through our daily ritual of flicking through the photos in my camera.

"What an incredible morning! I feel so privileged to be here and to have seen all that we've seen. It's been better than I imagined." I look at Gary and add, "Life is good, even with Parkinson's."

"You won't believe how good it is to hear you say that. You know the best part has been seeing you in your

Mary and Me

element, wind in your hair and in your happy place taking photos. I know holding your camera steady is frustrating for you, but I see your determination to find ways to make it work, and you have. It makes me more positive about what lies ahead."

"I can't wait to get home and turn the best shots into another photobook. If I ever end up in la-la land you have to show me my photobooks to remind me of the good life we've had."

"I don't like hearing you talk like that. There's nothing to say you will end up with dementia. Anyway, this experience is amazing, a big tick for the bucket list and I'm so grateful to be here." He fiddles with his phone. "Take a look at this. I've got some good video footage of the lion kill. There won't be much left of that zebra carcass for the hyenas."

I watch the video clip. "Wow, that's awesome. It really shows how hard life can be in the animal kingdom. Unless you're at the top of the food chain every day is a fight for survival, living on full alert while never knowing whether there's a predator lurking behind the next bush. It makes the stress in our lives look fairly benign."

"But we aren't guaranteed a life free of trials either. For the last month or so we've been fairly fixated on your Parkinson's, as if it's a predator that slowly devours its prey. But a fixation won't do us any good and it only adds to the stress. We need to get on and live each day to the max—to make the most of every day as much as we're able."

"You're right. I've allowed the fear to dominate and I've procrastinated. Now it's time for me to put it into perspective and to fight—not just talk about fighting, but to really fight like it's a fight for my survival."

"I once heard a soldier say that true courage is being scared but you go anyway. That's real bravery and I've always thought you are brave. You've demonstrated it many times, not least after you were assaulted."

"I guess in our context it's facing Parkinson's and fighting it every day."

He moves closer and puts his arm around my shoulders. "And I'm here to support you."

"I can do this. The fight starts today in earnest. Let's begin in the resort's gym." I turn to him and smile. "*Take that Parkinson's!*"

8

Mary, London, 1807

"Can't catch me," Mildred shouts.

Giggling, she runs around the table, her brown pigtails swinging and fat little arms flailing. As she scrambles to get around her grandmother she bumps her, causing ink to streak up the page of the ledger.

"Slow down!" Mary growls.

Three-year-old Mildred is no match for her five-year-old brother and Henry closes in. "Gotcha." He catches her by the arm and swings her around, knocking little Annie over. She lets out a wail. At just two years of age Annie tries hard to keep up with her older siblings.

"Shhh, you're not 'urt." Florence picks her up and brushes her knees. "Away from Grannie, go ou'side and play. Henry, take Annie with you and mind you look after 'er, you 'ear?"

Annie wriggles to get down and, once free, toddles over to Henry who takes her by the hand.

Mary turns her attention back to the accounts. The work has become difficult and painfully slow. Where once she took pride in the neat columns of numbers, they are now small and untidy, full of wiggles and collapsed loops.

Her left leg takes on a life of its own and begins to shake under the table, the heel tapping to make a din on the wooden floor. Only when she forces it down and thinks about it can she make it stop. Then almost as soon as she stops thinking about it the shaking starts up again.

The pen sits in the ink pot and she reaches for it with a trembling hand. Trying to grasp it she knocks the pot over, spilling ink over the table and splashing the page she's working on. She grabs some blotting paper to soak up the excess, but ugly smudges now make some of the numbers unreadable and Mary stares at the page, and weeps.

"Oooh, look at what you've done now," Florence says. "I told you to leave the book work to Edward."

Florence takes a rag from her apron and wipes the table, but ink has already stained the wood.

John hears the commotion and comes through from the shop. "What is all this fuss about?"

"I 'ad an accident with the ink, that's all." Mary uses her sleeve to soak up the tears.

"That's all? Woman, what is the matter with yer?"

"I-I don't know," she stammers. "I ain't able to stop me shakin'."

"Edward!" he calls.

Edward walks through from the shop.

"Edward, it's time you took over the accounts. Yer mother ain't capable of keeping the ledger. From now on, 'tis yer job."

"Yes, Father."

John eyes Mary with a cold expression. "Git away from them books, now. I don't want to see any more of this sort of ruckus." It's a command.

"I'm sorry." Her voice is no more than a whisper.

Mary and Me

John lowers his voice. "Whatever 'as a 'old on you needs to be contained."

He looks at her as if she is despicable and something withers inside her. Tears flow freely. She gets up from the table, climbs the stairs as fast as her legs will allow and flings herself on the bed. Her body heaves with sobs and she wonders what will become of her.

These past months have become more and more difficult. Not only does she have intense shaking, but she has become slow and clumsy. Florence now does the lion's share of both the shop and domestic chores, as well as raise her little ones, and Mary sees the resentment in her eyes. She wants to pull her weight in the way she always has. However, her body won't let her. Mary spills and drops, drools and freezes. Florence has had to clean up after her more than once in recent days.

She fears she is losing the respect of John. Any kindness he may have had for her is being replaced with a loathing. Her usefulness is now less than it was and she is fast becoming an embarrassment. Edward has always been her special boy, yet even he acts like she is a stranger. The tenderness he once showed has been replaced with a kind of confusion and he has distanced himself from her. They all fear her. She can see it in their eyes and she fears whatever it is that has a hold over her. Overcome with tiredness, her mind drifts.

A myriad of images flash about her, taunting her. Gargoyles, their grotesque faces being the image of evil itself, chase her. Punch and Judy puppets dance to a tremor. Other faces, partially hidden behind masks, jeer at her and mock her. Flames dance and lick her.

She wakes, unsure how long she has been asleep, and is desperate to shake off the dream. Nightmares are not new to her but of late they've become increasingly unsettling. Many a night she will wake from one and lie in the dark for hours, too afraid to go back to sleep. They fill her with dark thoughts that unsettle her, making her more and more morose. She struggles to lift her dark moods. Lately these terrifying visions have even come when she's awake. Her life has shifted to a world of shadows, one consumed by fear.

Her foot cramps with the toes painfully turned under like claws and she prises them open. Her arms and legs are stiff and ache as she gets up off the bed. At the dresser she pours a little water from the jug into the basin and uses it to splash her tear-streaked face. The clean skin feels fresh and tingly, but she knows she can't wash away the thing that plagues her.

Downstairs, she looks for ways to help Florence. Her condition renders her unable to help with very much at all. She has gone from managing the household, making the sweets, helping with the children and keeping the books, to just stirring pots and not a lot more.

Some jars are lined up on the table where they have been filled with biscuits. "Let me take them jars into the shop for you," Mary says.

Florence looks up from the pot she is stirring. "No need, I can do it meself."

"I want to 'elp."

"You just git under me feet. I prefer it when you stay in yer room." While Florence's reply is barely audible the words sting as if she has slapped Mary's face.

Mary and Me

Taking no notice Mary picks up a jar and, using both hands to hold it steady, carries it through to the counter. John and Edward are talking to one of the regular customers.

"Afternoon, Mrs Black." The woman's voice is overly sharp. She puts her arm out to her son who stands at her side and draws him near to her as if protecting him.

"Good afternoon, Mrs Porter, Jack. Lovely day out there today." Mary tries to sound upbeat, although her voice has become weak.

Mrs Porter looks nervously at John. "I 'ad better be goin' now, thank ye."

"But what about yer sweets?" he asks.

She eyes Mary and then turns back to John. "Maybe next time. Come Jack, let's not be loitering." She pushes her boy out the door and back onto the street.

"What do you think that was about?" Edward asks.

"I don't rightly know. Mighty strange if you ask me. She normally buys a generous amount."

Mary puts the jar in its place on the shelf and retreats to the kitchen for another. As she clasps the jar to her bosom her hand cramps like a claw with her thumb stuck between the second and third fingers. She ignores the pain and takes the jar through to the shelf beside the other one and not until it is on the shelf does she try to force the fingers open.

She shuffles back to the kitchen and picks up the last of the jars. Part way back to the shop counter she experiences something new. Her feet freeze and no matter how hard she tries to make one of them move forward, it twitches but remains frozen. It's as if it refuses to do as she commands. The shaking increases so she clutches the jar even tighter, determined not to drop it. With perseverance she takes a small step forward, and then another. Her steps are a mere shuffle, as though a thick wet blanket is wrapped tightly around her legs.

John watches her closely. "What's up with you, woman?"

"'Tis nothin', John."

"Why do you shake so much?" His tone is full of malice and she is afraid he thinks it is her own fault.

"I can't stop me shakin'. I wish I could. I just seem to 'ave no control over it."

He grunts.

An ominous foreboding comes over her as if someone has walked over her grave, and she shudders.

*

Several weeks have passed since the day Mary spilt the ink and was banned from keeping the books. The tiredness continues to dog her. The tremor is more relentless and she constantly experiences problems walking. Barely able to help Florence with the chores she frets that she is becoming a burden on the family.

Florence is making marzipan sweets and the little ones are playing upstairs. She is quiet and Mary leaves her to her brooding. It is normal for Florence to say little to Mary these days and when she does address her it is rarely charitable. Her tone and words are cold and sharp. Florence now sees their home and shop as her own domain and appears to have lost all respect for Mary as the matriarch.

Edward has the ledger spread out on the table and is fully absorbed. The handover of the task has been seamless and Mary is proud of his ability to make the neat rows of numbers. She has taught him well.

The little bell above the door to the shop sounds and Alice enters with some of her brood. John is in the shop and Mary can hear him begin to serve her. Mary shuffles through to join them.

"Top of the mornin' to you, Alice." Mary holds her arm behind her back in a futile attempt to conceal its tremor and her skirt hides the vibration in her leg.

Alice looks nervously at Mary before turning back to John.

"Alice?" Mary is baffled by her silent response.

She ignores Mary. "C'mon children, we best be off."

"But yer said we'd get sweets," the older boy wines.

"I ain't buying today." She hurries towards the door.

John asks, "Alice, whate'er is the matter? Pray tell."

"'Tis 'er." She pokes a fat finger towards Mary. "I'll not 'ave 'er infecting me children with 'er demons."

The words hit Mary hard and she stands rooted to the spot, her hand and leg shaking even more violently.

Alice hurries out of the shop, children in tow.

John looks at Mary. Their eyes lock briefly and in this moment she knows.

"That's twice this week we've lost a good customer." His eyes are hard and yet his voice betrays a note of pity.

"It ain't my fault. I don't know what to do, what to say." It is barely more than a whisper.

"It can't go on."

"I can't stop me shakin'. I only wish I could."

"'Tis as if the devil 'imself is inside of you." His face softens and his eyes plead with her. "Mary, you understand, don't you?"

She is too overcome to answer.

"Per'aps it's time you paid a visit to the vicar to get cleaned."

This man with whom she has born children believes her to be possessed. Maybe it isn't that surprising as even she has wondered the same, and perhaps she is. Her limbs seem to have a will of their own, as though they belong to someone else. What has she done to deserve this? *Lord forgive me*, she pleads silently.

She has heard the stories of folks possessed by demons who undergo the ritual of exorcism. It scares her and she would rather die than go to the church. Maybe it would be better to hide, somewhere she's not known, somewhere it won't reflect badly on the family.

"Mary." His voice is uncharacteristically full of emotion. "Mary, I ain't wanting this for you any more than you do. You must see this. As 'ead of this family I must do what's right for ev'ryone. We 'ave a business to run and we can't afford to 'ave customers too afraid to come in. We 'ave to keep bread on our table."

Her heart sinks. "I could 'ide upstairs an' only come out after the shop is closed."

"But what 'bout the nippers? What if it flies from you to them?"

"I could avoid 'em, take me meals upstairs."

John reaches his hand towards her and she tries not to flinch. He strokes her hair, his touch surprisingly gentle.

Mary and Me

"Mary, I 'aven't always been the best 'usband, but I've tried to provide for yer. You've always done well by me, raisin' Edward, keepin' the shop stocked and books up to date." He laughs and adds, "Yer smart for a woman, I'll grant yer that. You know this thing that 'aunts yer could be perilous for the family. Florence is doin' a fine job of keepin' 'ouse and stockin' the shop. Edward is good with 'em books. Yer don't need to worry about them things anymore."

"Maybe I should leave for the alms 'ouse," she says. "Might be best for ev'ryone." Although she says this she desperately wants him to tell her there is no need and everything will be okay.

Relief crosses his face. "Mary, I don't want to send yer there, but what choice do we 'ave? Where else is there?"

She is stricken to the depths of her soul. Her mind is numb and she can't trust herself to respond. Is she really hearing him? She has given this man not only her youth, but her life. Every waking moment for nearly thirty years she has fed him, washed for him, bore his children and raised their child, worked in his business. Everything he wanted of her, everything he needed of her, she gave willingly, asking for little in return. And now, when she's in desperate need of help, is he really saying he's prepared to turn his back on her? To cast her out? Tears flow down her cheeks and drip down to her bosom and she wipes them with her rag, not wanting to show her weakness.

"I'm so sorry," he says softly. When she doesn't respond he adds, "I need to think of what is best for me family. You understand, don't yer?"

130

She turns and shuffles towards the stairs, her head bent and tears flooding down her cheeks. Her body jerks and shakes and writhes; the monster within is becoming more powerful, more in control. She is merely his puppet. How she loathes this body and this thing that possesses her. How she wants to shrivel up and die. Why is this happening to her? What will become of her?

Reaching their chamber she climbs on the bed and an immense sorrow engulfs her. Sobs rack her body, sending shudders to meet the tremors. She holds herself with knees drawn up to her chest, rocking gently back and forth. And then she lets it out. She lets it all out. At first she doesn't recognise it, doesn't know where the sound comes from. A sound that could send fear through the coldest, toughest heart. Loud, long and shrill. A scream. It goes on and on. It is her.

And then there is silence.

*

Mary wakes and it is still dark outside. Loud snores provide a familiar backdrop to the black void of the night. She welcomes the refuge the darkness offers. Her mind is fully awake now. Her thoughts probe the depths of her awareness and it is all meaningless. Everything she has ever known turns out to be fleeting. Her family, her home, her work. Nothing is guaranteed. Nothing is trustworthy. It is like a wind through a meadow. One moment it is there and the next it is gone, with few signs to show where it has been.

She wonders if these are her own thoughts or the thoughts of the thing that moves her against her will.

Turning in bed has become more difficult and she struggles to reposition herself. Her toes are curled tightly under, causing painful cramps. She reaches down and tries to stretch them out.

Her heart is still disturbed by John's words from yesterday. His show of emotion and compassion stirred her and yet he left her in no doubt that she must make a grave decision, one that will affect the remainder of her life.

It is a terrible thing to realise you are no longer needed and, even worse, to be no longer wanted. For some time now she has sensed Florence's animosity, as if she's both embarrassed and resentful of Mary. Florence likes to be her own queen of the manor. She speaks with an acid tongue and Edward is no match for her. He has proven to be weak and allows her to treat his mother with contempt. Florence provides him with an ever-growing family and he is captivated by her.

Almost unwittingly, over a period of months, Mary has handed her responsibilities over to Florence and Edward as she has struggled to cope. The household and shop continue to run well without her. She had assumed this to be a temporary measure, that this thing that afflicts her would pass, but alas it continues to devour her more each day.

She listens to the heavy breathing beside her. He sleeps, oblivious to her dilemma. This man who wed her and bed her, prospered from her hard work and loyalty to him and their family. In return he shows no loyalty to her; merely a possession to be cast out. He is healthy and could easily replace her with another. Lord knows, there is many a widow who would choose him and this household over the poor house.

A woman who does not pull her weight in chores is dispensable and it would be better for everyone if she is no longer around. John is right. They must consider the welfare of the family first and do what will be best for them. This thing that afflicts her must not be passed to the others. That much is true. She must protect them from that. And it must not affect their ability to feed the growing family.

It is clear what she must do and she will do it before the family takes the decision from her. She will find a bed in one of the alms houses. From this day on she will live on charity, anonymously, so as not to bring further disrepute upon her family.

A loud snore erupts into the gloomy, pre-dawn light and blows out through loose lips. Mary plants a gentle kiss on her fingertips and lightly brushes it over her husband's lips, causing him to snuffle. The household retreats into silence and she is aware Florence will soon be up to begin the day's chores. If she is going to act it must be now before she weakens her resolve and before she must face Florence. She needs to hurry.

She sits up, taking a moment to absorb the light-headedness that so often plagues her, before lighting the candle. Her stiff limbs shake madly as she struggles to wash her withering body with the cold water from the jug. Once dry she dresses as hurriedly as she is able, layering the grey work dress over her one good dress before donning the apron. She brushes her tresses and secures the lace cap. On her feet she wears her boots that, although well worn, will be a great blessing in her new life. In a basket she places a candle, soap and hairbrush—all her possessions. The familiarity of the chamber in the dull candlelight causes her to tear up and she dabs her eyes with a rag, stifling a sob. She drops the rag into the basket, pulls the brown woollen shawl around her shoulders and makes her way downstairs as quietly as a church mouse.

In the shop she takes a nail and prises up the loose floorboard behind the counter. It squeaks and she freezes, listening for any sounds above. All is quiet. She lets her breath out and gently lifts the wooden box from its hiding place. Opening it she takes out five shillings before carefully putting it back and replacing the floorboard. With a last lingering look around the sweet shop she loves she blows out her candle and drops it into the basket with the coins. When she opens the door the little bell jingles above her for the last time.

9

Rose, Tauranga, April 2017

After arriving home from East Africa I contacted Parkinson's New Zealand and arranged to meet with their community educator. It's the first real step towards starting my campaign to fight this thing that began when those two little words were spoken over me.

The doorbell rings.

I check my watch and hurry down the stairs and open the door to an older woman.

"Rose?"

"Yes, and you must be Yvonne. Come on in."

The community educator from Parkinson's New Zealand kicks off her shoes and follows me inside and up the stairs to where Gary is waiting.

They shake hands and introduce themselves. She comes across as a motherly type, with a lined, round face that is warm and friendly. I take an instant liking to her.

"I'm here to tell you what help is available to you and I can answer any questions or concerns you might have about Parkinson's."

We nod.

"It's been a bit of a shock. We've had experience with Parkinson's disease as my auntie had it and I visited her in a rest home most weeks until she passed away." There's a tremor in my voice and the all-too-familiar tears well up. I add quietly, "It was awful."

Yvonne's face softens as she looks from me to Gary. "The first thing you need to know is that every patient with Parkinson's is unique. I deal with many patients and I can honestly say I have not come across two who present in exactly the same way. The combination of symptoms varies. The speed of progression and the way people react to drugs can also be different. You mustn't think your disease will necessarily be like that of your aunt's."

I take in a long, slow breath and feel the tension ease.

Yvonne asks about my symptoms and takes notes as I describe my journey. I begin with the intermittent tremor and how it became persistent with time, the misdiagnosis when visiting the first neurologist and the spread of the tremor into my left leg. I tell her I went to another neurologist for a second opinion and got the Parkinson's diagnosis. I finish my narrative describing my stiffness in the mornings and how it takes time to get my body going, symptoms I'd thought were part of normal ageing.

"Have you had the shoulder pain yet?"

"Why?" I can hear the surprise in my voice.

"Many of my clients complain about pain in their shoulders."

"Interesting." I lean forward. "I've had two frozen shoulders in the last two years and they haven't responded well to treatment. They've stopped me playing squash. I hadn't considered this could be related to Parkinson's."

"Do you have any problems with constipation?"

I describe my history of poor gut health in excruciating detail—the diagnosis of irritable bowel syndrome at

21, my bouts of pain and poor appetite, catching Montezuma's Revenge in Mexico in the nineties, the numerous colonoscopies and my overly sensitive gut. I tell her I took antibiotics continuously for seven years as a child for a deep lung infection and that this could have led to my gut problems. As I speak, Yvonne nods encouragement and continues to take notes.

"What about your bladder function?"

"Well, when I need to go, I need to go—now." I grimace, thinking about the times I make a mad dash for the bathroom. "But it's manageable and not a problem."

"How well do you sleep?"

"I used to be an eight-hour-a-night girl, but for some time now I've been waking in the early hours, usually any time after two a.m. and I struggle to get back to sleep. Is it related to Parkinson's?"

"It can be a symptom. I see a lot of patients who have sleep issues."

"I thought it was a disease affecting movement," Gary says.

"That's what most people think, but there's a lot more to it." She rifles through her bag and produces a brochure. "I'll leave this with you. It's a good read and explains the symptoms well."

"Thanks."

She changes tack to ask what drugs I'm on, advising me to consult my doctor with any concerns. "Do you have any questions for me?"

"No, not really." My mind feels like a blank canvas.

"What about you, Gary?"

"I'm still processing. We've talked already about Rose giving up her work and focusing on fighting the disease. Her specialist said to make exercise the most important thing in her day and that requires time and energy. I also want her to avoid unnecessary stress."

"That's very sensible, if you can do it. Stress is known to make it worse." Yvonne turns to me. "What work do you do?"

"I'm a solo business consultant, working mostly with corporates. I also do a bit of governance work."

"Sounds like it could be stressful."

"I love it and I like to think I thrive on stress. But this diagnosis has made me rethink what's important." A catch in my voice betrays my calm as the image of Margaret comes to mind and I have to fight to retain control. "My auntie went downhill fairly quickly after she was diagnosed. I may not have many healthy years left and we need to make the most of what we have while we can still enjoy them."

Gary winces, his eyes brim with tears. "Don't say that." His voice is husky.

"It's true though and we need to face it. I'm sick and it's going to get worse."

"You're no sicker than you were before the diagnosis and that wasn't that long ago." His voice is soft, a gentle reminder.

"That's true. But we need to plan for a different future now. We can't bargain on years of good health anymore."

"Let's just take one year at a time."

Yvonne had put her pen down and was watching our interchange with interest. "There's often a honeymoon period of a few years after diagnosis when you maintain good health."

"I need more than a few years." The words come out a little too fast. "I'm sorry, I don't mean to sound rude."

"You don't. It's normal to grieve for the loss of a healthy body. Most patients go through a grief cycle after diagnosis. Are you familiar with the grief cycle?"

"A little," I say.

"You can expect to go through denial, anger, guilt or thinking if only you'd done something differently, and even depression, before you can really accept the condition. Having a diagnosis for Parkinson's disease means a lot of change and an uncertain future. Most people find that pretty scary. It can affect relationships, any plans for your future as well as your income. It's a lot to deal with."

I don't answer. I can't answer. I focus on a mark on the wall, willing myself to be strong and determined not to show the emotional rollercoaster inside my head.

"Diet and exercise are important treatments," Yvonne continues. "Are you interested in being part of a clinical diet trial? There's one starting at Waikato Hospital to test the effects of two different diets on Parkinson's disease. I hear they're looking for more patients to sign up."

"Sure, that would really interest me."

"I'll email you the information when I get home. I run support groups for people with Parkinson's. You might like to come along. I generally have a topic and then allow time for social interaction. It's a good chance to get to know others and hear how they are coping with the disease." Yvonne pulls a paper out of her bag and hands it to me. She turns to Gary. "There's also a carers' group."

Gary and I exchange glances.

"I'm not Rose's carer. I see myself as her supporter. She doesn't need a carer."

Yvonne looks embarrassed. "No, of course not."

"To be honest, I really don't want to go to events with other Parkinson's patients, at least not yet. I don't need to be confronted with reminders of what my future might look like." Not wanting to sound rude, I add, "Maybe later."

"That's entirely up to you. I'll keep you up to date with what's on and you're welcome to join us at any time."

"Thanks."

We finish our meeting with the usual pleasantries and I see Yvonne out.

"That was worthwhile." Gary looks up as I come back in.

"Mmm, lots to think about, and so much we don't know."

"You were going to spend some time in research."

"I know. I just need to find the time." I look at him and hold his gaze for a moment. "We need to talk about our future. Perhaps we should book in a meeting with our lawyer."

"Whatever for?" He pulls his brows into a frown.

"What if," I say, then add in a quiet voice, "I need to go into a rest home like Margaret."

"No, we are not discussing this."

"It's no good being in denial. We have to consider all possibilities." I push on, ignoring the crushed look on his face. "We've saved for our retirement to live the dream in our so-called golden years. Now it's highly likely those years won't be so golden, at least not for us. If I have to go prematurely into a rest home it'll cost all of our savings. You'll still be relatively young and there'll be nothing left for you to enjoy."

Tears escape down his cheeks and I know I've hit a raw nerve. "I don't want to discuss this. Not now and, preferably, not ever."

I ignore him. "Our savings will be mined until there is virtually nothing left. It's just how it was for your parents."

"I don't care about the money. I care about what happens to you. We can face those scenarios if they ever happen, but that'll be decades away."

"But it's not fair on you. It's almost inevitable that I will end up needing care and it's no good putting our heads in the sand." I focus on a spot on the wall to stop my eyes from welling up.

"If you ever need care I'd rather care for you here in our own home than send you to a rest home. It may not be a lot more to get part-time nursing care into our home than to pay for hospital-level care in an institution."

"We would need to sell this house and move, to avoid stairs. There'll come a time when I won't be able to manage them. I like the idea of being able to stay at home, especially if there's a view. I'd like to have something to watch all day. I hate the idea of being in a room with a whole lot of people who are suffering as Margaret did."

"You don't need to, and you heard Yvonne say everyone with Parkinson's is unique in the way it manifests itself. You are not your auntie."

"No, I'm not. I'm just trying to be pragmatic."

"I need to get back to work." He takes my hands and raises them to his lips. "You have to stop thinking negative thoughts. It won't do you any good."

"I'm not seeing the glass half empty. I'm just trying to be realistic. We really do need to prepare for whatever lies ahead."

"Whatever it is we'll face it together. You've already had these symptoms a long time and you were doing well before the diagnosis. Why should that suddenly change?"

"You're right. There's just so much to take in." I give his hand a squeeze. "I'll start my own literature review. I'll also find out more about the diet trial."

"Now that sounds more like you. You're a fighter and not one to give in easily. That's one of the many things I love about you." His face breaks into an impish grin. "You fight this and you could become the pin-up girl for Parkinson's."

It is good to laugh at the one thing that has caused us so much torment in these past few months.

*

To live well with Parkinson's will be a challenge and I need to give myself the best possible chance to either beat it or slow down its advance until such time as a cure is available. If I'm serious about fighting it, from what I've learned so far, I'll have to do so on multiple fronts. I need to go into battle pre-armed and, with every possible weapon in my arsenal, I will give it my all.

I sit at my keyboard, my fingers poised on the keys. I need to know exactly what I'm dealing with and be smart about it. I type some key words into the browser. 'Doctor' Google has loads of information. The trick is to sift the wheat from the chaff. It should be safe to assume reputable medical journals, neurological foundation websites and Parkinson's organisations are the most credible sources. The web is full of information and I learn new terms, like dopamine, substantia nigra, dyskinesia, bradykinesia, dystonia, Lewy bodies, neuroplasticity... The list goes on.

Essentially, Parkinson's disease causes dopamine-producing neurons to die, in the substantia nigra part of the midbrain. This is the part of the brain that controls reward and movement. Hence the mood disorders, the lethargy and the abnormal movements. These neurons have been found to have a build-up of protein matter called Lewy bodies, now widely thought to be the cause of neurons dying.

It's generally accepted that it starts in either the gut or the olfactory gland and, as I have a keen sense of smell, mine must have started in the gut and moved into the brain. It's strange to see the gut referred to as the second brain. It can affect the autonomic nervous system that controls the automatic functioning of various organs, giving rise to a wide range of symptoms, such as low blood pressure, urinary problems and bowel function. The possible symptoms just go on and on. No wonder we all have our own unique set of them. Parkinson's is like a sleepy hippo submerged in the river; the motor symptoms are what you see, but the bulk of the symptoms are hidden from view.

I come across a study that links the prolonged use of antibiotics to Parkinson's disease. Those seven years of antibiotics may have been one of the contributing factors for me. If only we'd known then what we now know about the potential harm in prescribing their long-term use. Neither

Mary and Me

did we know back then to accompany them with probiotics and prebiotics.

I find a Canadian report linking Parkinson's with survivors of hanging and strangulation and wonder if this could also be a contributing factor for me.

I continue my search. Parkinson's is a tricky disease and even though a lot of research has gone into finding a cure they are still no closer to solving it. The disease is more of a syndrome, made complex because of multiple sub-types yet to be classified. This could explain the variation in symptoms, motor and non-motor, and the different factors that are believed to cause it. One thing that's clear is how common it is. Everyone probably knows somebody affected by it.

I read several quotes stating that even though the disease is degenerative and has no cure people generally don't die of it. They die with it. If these quotes are meant to be positive they do nothing to pull me out of my increasingly morbid mood.

My specialist discussed with me a procedure called deep brain stimulation where they can insert a probe into the brain and hook it up to a battery pack. For most patients it can reduce the tremor. It's high risk and, for me at my stage, the risks outweigh the benefits. He said it could be an option for me later when the disease has advanced, making the tremor more debilitating. I enter the words into the browser and numerous references appear. It sounds like a game of Russian Roulette, but one day it could be a lifeline for me and I know I'll be willing to give it a go.

A link to a story about epilepsy and neuroplasticity comes into my browser and I click on it. It's a curious story about a woman who suffers from epilepsy and who is now a successful photographer. After experiencing extreme episodes of fitting she underwent an operation to have half her brain removed; the lobe damaged from prolonged fitting. Over time the remaining brain adapted and began to perform tasks that normally would be controlled by the lobe that was removed. It's an inspirational story and something resonates with me.

In need of a break I consider getting some exercise. Perhaps I could try Gary's rowing machine or the treadmill downstairs. He also has a resistance trainer, a frame with bungys for strength training, that now has a thinner bungy cord especially for me, but I keep putting off using it. The mere thought makes me feel fatigued and I decide on a caffeine hit instead. Today might be better spent continuing my research while I'm on a roll. I can always exercise tomorrow. It's an excuse. Avoiding exercising worsens my lethargy and it's hard to push through that barrier of perpetual tiredness.

In the kitchen I go through my coffee ritual. As I put the coffee pot on the gas hob my mind continues to absorb the information from my research. The story of the lady with epilepsy dominates my thoughts. If her brain could adapt to the loss of a lobe why can't mine adapt to the loss of dopamine-producing neurons? I need to understand more about this neuroplasticity. Does it hold the key to fighting Parkinson's? My spirit lifts as I grab hold of this thread of hope.

Coffee in hand, I settle back into the study and dive back down the rabbit hole.

Neuroplasticity is an interesting concept and its application to Parkinson's patients seems to be fairly recent. It's about teaching the brain to change its structure and function in response to activity and mental experiences. Other stories surface relating to Parkinson's patients finding ways to compensate for movement. The more I read, the more fascinated I become and I know I'm on to something. It makes so much sense. The idea that we use only a fraction of our brain suggests we have spare neurons yet to be commissioned. If that's true, then how can we commission unused healthy ones to replace the dopamine-producing cells that are now defunct? Perhaps to commission my spares I need to teach myself new and complex movements, movements I have no memory for, that are new to my body—like different dance or combat formats.

I shut down my browser, now with more questions than answers. Neuroplasticity. I like the sound of the word and I roll it around like a sweet melody. It's a word filled with hope and I leave my study with renewed purpose, knowing my journey is just beginning.

*

Consciousness dawns slowly as I become aware of intense pain in my arm and I wriggle to find a comfortable position. I have been plagued by a dull ache in my shoulder that extends into my upper arm muscle, but this is different. The pain runs the length of my arm and, as I move my elbow, it is almost unbearable. I haven't injured it and it's too intense to be from lying on it. Maybe there is no cause, no injury, no source, just confused pain sensors. I lie flat on my back, my arm flat and straight, trying to blot it out. It is still dark. I listen for the dawn chorus or the distant commuter cars. It's quiet and I know it's too early.

There is no pain! Still I feel it.

As always at this hour my Parkinson's is a foreboding presence. It comes wrapped in fear. It's only during these early and lonely hours when I'm at my weakest that it gets to rob me of my fortitude, my joy.

My mind drifts to memories of Auntie Margaret. The first time we noticed something odd was when she invited us over for dinner. She used to be a competent and a great hostess, but on this occasion it appeared the meal had been too much for her and she was not coping well. At the time we thought she must have been drunk. However, it wasn't long after that evening that she told us she had Parkinson's. Margaret was always a great walker and she liked to roam the hills. Yet even her fitness couldn't hold back the Parkinson's and it progressed rapidly. She didn't have much of a tremor, but her movements became very slow and she suffered numerous falls that resulted in several trips to hospital. She became quite confused and eventually went into care, which she hated. Her body had frozen and she was unable to converse. Even eating became an issue with the risk of choking.

O Lord, I do not want to end like that.

Tears well up. These days my emotions are close to the surface, another Parkinson's trait. I try to keep these moments to myself so I'm strong for my family. I need to think of more positive things. It's my only defence.

I make a mental list of my weapons—prayer, positive thinking, pills, diet and exercise. I play with forming an acronym, a mind game to pass the time. PPPDE won't do. Rearranging the letters I come up with PEPPD and smile. PEPPD to fight, with p̲rayer, e̲xercise, p̲ositive thinking, p̲ills and d̲iet. Perfect!

I wish I could simply take a pill to cure this disease, but there isn't one. The pills on offer only help with the symptoms. I've been taking pills for three months now and my tremor is only marginally better compared to before I was diagnosed. Pills alone will not win the battle but every bit of progress helps.

It's become a priority to get rid of the pain in my shoulders. A trip to my physio with Gary had her teach him how to get rid of the knots in my upper back and shoulders. Now he's on his way to becoming an expert masseur, so much so that our last purchase online was a massage table to stop me suffocating when my nose was pressed hard into the mattress. A personal masseur along with the prescribed painkillers and anti-inflammatories are part of the solution. The more important part is more exercise.

I need a routine to combat the apathy. Otherwise, it's too easy to fool myself into thinking a day off won't hurt and I can catch up on exercise tomorrow. Setting aside time each day, before I do any work, for massage, stretching, gentle strength training and some form of cardio exercise might be a good idea. If I rule that time out in my diary it may give me the best shot at resisting the apathy.

I will fight. I pray, thankful for my life and desperate to receive more strength to embolden my fight.

Neuroplasticity. That word again. Not long ago I hadn't even heard of it and now it seems vitally important.

The stories randomly roll around like shapes in a kaleidoscope.

Finally, dawn approaches and the alarm sounds. Gary wakes and rolls towards me, pulling me in to his arms. "Good morning," he mumbles into my neck. "Want to join me in the garage for a workout before breakfast?"

"I've had another bad night. I woke up with fairly intense pain, this time in my arm. I'm sure I haven't injured it. Perhaps my pain sensors are a bit scrambled. I've been awake for ages though, so I'm a bit jaded."

"Are you okay now?"

"It's eased off now. I've been thinking. Remember that TED Talk about the Parkinson's man and the stairs?"

"That was really interesting. What about it?"

I snuggle further into his arms. "I've read some other patients' stories, such as the one where a man struggled to walk without a walker and yet he could bounce a football on his foot with normal fluid movements. And another who suffered severe freezing when walking could ride a bike without any problems."

"What do you make of them?"

"These stories all point to similar outcomes—people with Parkinson's who are able to compensate for their immobility. Maybe it's possible to find a strategy to bypass the problem area in the brain."

"Sounds like outwitting the symptoms."

"Exactly. If we could be innovative in our response to any movement issues that might develop I could stay mobile. I think it's about switching from the automated movements like walking to more deliberate movements."

"If the time comes, and I mean *if*, we should experiment with different strategies and see what will work for you."

"Why wait? If I start now perhaps I can pre-empt the problems and put solutions in place. I think that's the key to neuroplasticity."

"Maybe so. It's certainly worth experimenting. But for now, we agreed you'd start getting serious about exercise. You can't keep procrastinating."

"Okay, let's do it. I'll need to build up slowly to avoid more injuries."

We head downstairs in our gym gear and warm up together. I spend ten minutes on the rowing machine, but my lethargy is bad, my legs ache and it's just too hard. I give up and try the resistance trainer. It's an easy workout focused on strength-building exercises for my shoulders and upper back. I can't help being discouraged as I've lost so much strength, but it's a start and I know there's a lot of work to do to regain my range of movement, if it's even possible. Whatever happened to that girl who was full of vitality and who loved nothing more than a hard game of squash?

Gary is still on the treadmill when I traipse back upstairs. I stand under the shower, allowing the water to stream over me and wash away my fears and disappointment. The mountain seems huge, so hard to climb, but there is no choice. It will be one step at a time.

10

Rose, Tauranga, May 2017

I sit at my laptop filling out the diary I've started to track my symptoms and interventions, when it chimes to signal a new email landing in my inbox. I flick between screens and see it's from a neurologist at Waikato Hospital. It's an invitation to join a group of Parkinson's patients in an introductory meeting for the dietary trial at the hospital. It appears I'm a late addition and so before the week is out I head to Hamilton.

As I enter the hospital grounds I peer through the windscreen. Rain droplets form rivulets and race against the uncompromising wipe of the wiper blades. I drive into the hospital carpark and up the ramp, around and up, around and up. I take the last carpark on the roof and try to dodge the now persistent rain as I make for the lifts. Once it would have been a mad dash, but having sat in the car for an hour my legs don't respond to my urge to hurry and I arrive drenched.

Through a maze of corridors I find my way to the neurology department and take a seat in the waiting room. I can easily pick out the other Parkies waiting as if we have a label stamped on our foreheads. It's the wide unblinking eyes, the bradykinesia or slow movements, the dyskinesia or abnormal movements and, of course, the tremors.

Mary and Me

A youngish man in a long-sleeved blue check shirt tucked into his belted jeans and carrying a plunger full of black coffee calls us by name. We follow the coffee aroma—that is those of us who have retained our sense of smell—into a small room where Matt, the neurologist, introduces himself. We Parkies number eight, both men and women, and we each take a seat in the chairs spaced in a strategic semi-circle around Matt. I look like the youngest in this group and, judging by the involuntary movements around me, probably have the least advanced disease.

Matt begins with a brief overview of the disease and why he believes diet could help. The way he tells it makes perfect sense. Many Parkinson's cases start in the gut, making diet an obvious contender when looking for an intervention. The mitochondria are the powerhouse in the cells and they typically get their energy from glucose in the carbohydrates and proteins, but they can also burn ketones from fats.

"I get frustrated seeing my Parkinson's patients and knowing I can't do more for them. The traditional drugs are good, but they aren't a cure and they don't take away all the symptoms. I believe we need a more holistic approach, more tools to improve the quality of life for our patients." He pours more coffee into his now empty mug and waves his plunger pot at us. "Would anyone like a coffee? There's no milk or sweetener so I can only offer it black."

I look at the thick, black coffee left in the plunger and at this doctor who shows more interest in us as people and less as subjects to study. Three of us order coffee and we wait for Matt to source mugs and make a fresh pot. I could definitely work with this coffee lover.

"We are what we eat." He pauses to survey the room. "And I believe diet could be a significant key to Parkinson's clinical care."

Another thread of hope.

"There've been some studies overseas that show promise, but what is needed is a trial to prove that diet will provide real clinical benefits. People have said it can't be done with Parkinson's patients, that they couldn't be expected to stick to a strict dietary plan. I think together we can do it."

A murmur runs around the room as we look at one another, acknowledging we are up for the challenge.

Matt grins and continues, "We are looking for fifty Parkinson's patients who are willing to join a dietary trial. There are two diets; the ketogenic one with high fat and low carbs and the other with low fat and high carbs. Protein is to be standardised across both groups. Participants will be randomly selected and allocated one of these diets."

My interest is piqued, hoping for the keto diet.

"We will give you a shopping list, a meal plan and the precise recipes. You will need to commit to following the plan for the length of the trial. I will provide you with some videos to help you prepare the meals. I am working with a dietitian and we will be available to you at any time if you have any concerns or questions. I have two other neurologists who will assess you clinically; before, midway through and at the end of the trial."

Something about Matt appeals to me. Perhaps it's his open and casual manner. His enthusiasm for a more holistic approach to treatment is refreshing. As I listen I

Mary and Me

find myself drawn in, wanting to do my part to help, so by the end of the meeting I'm ready to sign on the dotted line.

In six weeks Matt will reveal to each of us which diet we've been allocated. Our baseline data will be assessed and the trial will start.

*

Slowly I pull myself out of my drowsiness and reach for my phone on the little bedside table. Its glow sends eerie light into the darkness as I flip its case open and see it is six fifteen a.m.—nearly time to get up. I've slept a full eight hours. Gary shifts next to me, momentarily disturbed by my movements. His slow, deep breathing tells me he's still asleep and I snuggle into him.

Today is my birthday and I intend to celebrate. I'm guessing Gary will take me out for a nice meal somewhere tonight. It's also the last day of the Parkinson's ketogenic diet clinical trial and I'm meeting with the team running it. I'm excited about this as I've carefully followed the prescribed diet and I can't wait to see the results. It's been a challenge—following recipes, weighing all ingredients, cooking two different meals and buying two sets of groceries—but I think the benefits outweigh the hassles. I'm a lot better and can only put it down to the diet.

"Happy birthday." Gary kisses me. "I got you a little something."

He opens the drawer in his bedside cabinet and pulls out a small box wrapped in gift paper and a card. I open the card first and it shakes as I read the words penned in his familiar style: *In sickness and in health, I wouldn't have it any other way. I love you.* My eyes moisten as I recognise the depth of his love for me, knowing that nothing is going to change that. I tear the blue and white spotted paper and open the box to reveal a Polar fitness watch.

"Oh, thank you. What a great present!"

"I thought it would be. This will allow you to track your physical activity and enable you to set yourself goals for your exercise programme." He picks up a small piece of paper now lying on the discarded wrapping paper, covered with writing in a minute font that would challenge those with the best of eyesight. "You'll need this to work out how to set it up. I chose one that will monitor your heart rate as well as distance, elevation, time, speed, etcetera."

"It's so perfect, thanks." I reach over and place it and the card on my bedside table, then pull him to me. Words are inadequate to describe the love I have for this man.

Later, I pull into the carpark at Waikato Hospital. My new watch, now fully charged, is displayed on my wrist. My mood is upbeat as I tread the now familiar route to the neurology department. I sign in and take my place in the waiting area.

Matt comes out and his grin is infectious as he comes over to me.

"Come on through. You can get underway by having your bloods taken. How've you been?"

"Really good. I'm sure I'm feeling better. The tremor isn't any different, but I've got more energy, I'm sleeping better, my gut health is behaving and I like to think my cognitive function is sharper."

"Whoa! Let's put you through the process and see how you fare. I'll see you when you're all done."

In a small office the nurse takes my bloods, tests my blood pressure and makes her notes. Next is the neurologist's assessment. He is what is termed a blind neurologist as he knows nothing about me nor what diet I'm on. He puts me though my paces and, as was instructed, I am careful not to offer him any more information than what he asks. Matt has been at pains to ensure we do nothing to bias the results. Next is the detailed questionnaire which asks all manner of questions about my current health and symptoms. These range from sleep to mood to bladder function to bowel function to pain and so on. After the tests are completed I wait for Matt to call me into his office.

"Come on in and take a seat." Matt flicks through some papers. "How's it been?"

"Well, I've stuck to the diet, 100 per cent. I haven't cheated once. As I said earlier, I'm generally feeling much more like my old self, with more vitality. I can't say that my tremor is any better, at least not significantly so. Is it true that I've probably already lost 70 per cent of my dopamine cells and I can't get those back?"

"By the time the motor symptoms take hold it's estimated that between 35 to 70 per cent of the dopamine-producing cells are lost and then you could expect to lose two per cent per year or twenty per cent over ten years. I can tell you your improvement while on the diet is 47 per cent in the comprehensive Parkinson's scores, virtually halving the severity over the last two months." Matt is talking quickly as he rattles these numbers off.

"Really? Wow, that's really encouraging."

"Extrapolating this out, it means you could slow down the deterioration by as much as one per cent per year, maybe even more."

The thread of hope I had attached to the diet grows into a cord.

"It's my birthday today and that is the best present I could have. That's so awesome. Thanks so much for giving me the chance to take part in your trial."

Matt looks pensive as he picks up his coffee mug and takes a drink. "You have done so well. These results are very significant, way better than any placebo effect and I'm very grateful to you for making the effort and maintaining the diet. In fact, all the participants have done well. The fallout rate is very low for a trial of this type."

"You made it easy for us and I'm sure no one would have wanted to let you down. We know how hard it is for you to get funding for your work."

"The trial has gone so well that I'm hoping to extend it. I haven't secured the funding yet, but would you be keen? We need to understand how far we can push the results and how permanent the changes might be."

"Absolutely yes. In fact I'd already decided to carry on with the diet. Do you think it's possible to manage my symptoms with diet and exercise alone, to live well without the drugs?"

"Well, it is a degenerative disease and there's certainly a place for drugs when managing the symptoms. I believe it's wise to take a holistic approach and diet is part of that. We are entering unchartered waters. The results from the trial are better than what we see from many drug trials. If you are keen to continue I'll arrange to get you more ketone and glucose strips so you can continue to monitor the levels in your blood."

"Sure, put me down as a definite starter."

"Great. Look, you should be very encouraged. Frankly, your results are extremely good." He beams his easy smile. "Happy birthday!"

I thank him and wish him luck, then head for the car. I couldn't be happier. My phone rings as I leave the carpark and it's Lauren calling to wish me a happy birthday. I share my good news with her. She and Paul recently moved back to New Zealand and I'm loving having my daughter in the same country again.

I drive home in a buoyant mood, my favourite music pumping. I shower and change into going-out clothes, taking time over my hair and makeup. It's to be a date night and I want to look my best. It's not long before I hear Gary's car zoom up the drive.

We sit in a restaurant, not like those bored-looking couples who have used up all their words and have nothing left to say, not like those who prefer their phone's social media to their date, but as two people who enjoy each other's company. The atmosphere is congenial, lights are dim and contemporary jazz music provides soft background sound.

We chat about our day and the waiter interrupts to take our orders. The menu doesn't cater for keto diets. I order the steak and ask that the chef holds the carbs. He comes back a minute later to say the chef will do a blue cheese sauce for the steak and add an extra helping of vegetables. It doesn't happen at all restaurants and I express my appreciation for the chef who is willing to accommodate my diet.

I tell Gary all I learned at the hospital.

"I am really hopeful that I can slow the disease down through strict diet and exercise. The results are undeniable. It really is a possibility. I can do this. I'm ready to throw everything at it. Even though I've always talked about fighting it this now gives me some real tangible hope."

He looks bemused.

"What?" I ask.

"It seems like ages since you've been this excited."

"I can't help it, I am excited. To be honest, it's the first time since being diagnosed that I feel like I can slow it down and live well until such time as they find a cure. Even if that's ten years away we can manage this thing. I really believe in this concept of neuroplasticity. I've been reading about a South African man with Parkinson's who's developed a type of conscious walking whereby he's trained himself to walk focusing on the muscle groups as they control the movement. He reckons it's helped his symptoms, but the only problem is when he stops his walking for any length of time the symptoms come back. It's an example of neuroplasticity. I'd argue, however, it's unidimensional."

"What do you mean by that?"

"Even though Margaret was fit and regularly went for long, fast walks up and down the hills, her Parkinson's rapidly got worse. You could argue she wasn't employing neuroplasticity and yet she was certainly fit. I've been squash fit and squash requires you to think strategically during rallies, but my tremor continued to increase. So fitness, even fitness combined with complex thinking, doesn't appear to be enough."

"But perhaps your squash has slowed the onset down."

"Maybe it has. We can never know that for sure. I've been thinking that I need to teach myself new complex movements as part of the fitness programme."

"Sounds credible. How would you do that?"

"I'm not sure yet, but maybe through dance, Pilates, karate or boxing. Lots of possibilities. I just need to work out how to do it on the cheap. I could combine it with cardio and strength training for all-round fitness. That's what I'd call multi-dimensional fitness."

"Why don't you check out the internet? It must have some routines."

"Good idea. After talking to Matt I've set myself a goal to become drug free with diet and exercise. It may not be possible, but I'm willing to give it a try. Perhaps the combination of these things will make a real difference."

He reaches over to take my hand. "That's such good news. I've also been thinking. We should plan an early retirement and just take off and do the stuff we've always planned we'd do. Besides, it's not just your Parkinson's. Either one of us could get sick and we could miss out on a healthy retirement together. One of the positive things to come out of your diagnosis is learning to live for today and enjoying our health and all the blessings we have."

The waiter arrives with two plates of steaming food and Gary quickly releases my hand. The waiter wishes us "bon appetit" before heading back to the kitchen.

"Could we really afford for us both to retire early?"

"It would mean spending the kids' inheritance. We could buy a campervan and become gypsies. We've always talked about doing the UK and Europe in a campervan.

Why not simply bring it forward? We could rent out the house and live off the rent, at least until we get a pension."

"That's worth exploring. Wouldn't it be awesome if we could?" I stop to chew on a forkful of food. "Mmm, this is absolutely delicious."

"This is also superb." He points his fork at the lamb hock sitting on his plate. "I'll run some numbers on it. None of us are guaranteed tomorrow, so from now on let's make the most out of the years we have. Isn't that why we worked so hard in our earlier years? For such a time as this?"

We continue to dream and scheme while enjoying the delicious food. It's the perfect end to a perfect birthday. *So, take that Parkinson's!*

*

Today is Christmas Day and we have all the family home to help celebrate. It's a time I should cherish yet I wake up on edge. Cooking has always come easy to me, but these days cooking for larger numbers seems to be unusually stressful and being a perfectionist I want to create the perfect meal.

I've decided to give up the keto diet, mainly to make life easier and because Gary and I are planning to take a sailing holiday in the new year. Keto on a yacht is just too hard to maintain as there won't be ready access to fresh produce and carbs are far easier to store. The keto diet flicked a switch for me in terms of my gut health. Now I hope to maintain the benefits with a healthy Mediterranean style diet with minimal processed foods and no added sugar, since both trial groups had low sugar and both showed some improvement in symptoms.

The house is buzzing with the usual Christmas excitement. Between mouthfuls of cereal I begin to prepare the desserts. First up is a pavlova, a family favourite. I break the first egg and the half-shell in my left hand begins to shake, piercing the yolk as I try to separate it from the white. A little yolk falls into the bowl with the egg white. I get a spoon and manage to pick out the streaks of yellow.

I successfully separate the second egg, and the third. But my tremor causes the fourth yolk to break and smears of yellow filter throughout the whites. Again I try to remove it, but there's too much to get it all. I dump the bowl of whites into the sink and curse my tremor.

"Mum, what is it?" Lauren comes to my side and, seeing me wash away the eggs, she asks, "Why have you tipped the eggs out?"

"My stupid tremor has ruined the pavlova." I fight back my tears.

"Here, let me do it for you." She reaches for the bowl.

"No, I need to do it. Please don't rescue me."

"But Mum, it's just a dessert." She is clearly surprised by my outburst.

"I don't care. I need to do this myself. I will do it." It's harsher than intended and she looks upset. "I'm sorry, but I have to keep doing things myself. I can't let the tremor stop me."

"Okay, I'll leave you to it." She hurries out of the kitchen and I know I've hurt her. Part of me wants to follow her and explain my frustration, part wants to let her take over the cooking. I stubbornly dry the bowl and start again.

I finally have pure egg white to beat, although not without more failures and time picking out little blobs of yolk. I slowly beat in the sugar, then the other ingredients, pile it on the tray and put it in the oven.

The family are somewhat subdued in the lounge and I realise they are all aware of my frustration and are walking on eggshells. I decide to try harder and make amends.

"Hey, I'm sorry about my outburst. Sometimes the frustration of not being able to do simple everyday tasks gets to me. I just want everything to be perfect for Christmas."

"Perhaps you should accept some help," Gary says.

"Christmas dinner can be a team effort," Lauren says. "We all want to help."

"I know, you're right. I feel like I'm on a rat wheel and just have to keep going. If I stop I'm scared I might not get going again."

Lauren comes over and gives me a hug. "It's okay Mum. You tell us what you want us to do and I promise I won't try to rescue you."

"Thank you. I promise to try and keep my frustration under wraps."

The doorbell sounds.

"I'll go." Michael is on his feet and runs down the stairs before anyone else can react.

Dad comes into the room. "Merry Christmas everyone."

We all exchange Christmas greetings and Lauren helps me to bring out some drinks and snacks.

"Rose, I've got something exciting to show you." Dad passes me a piece of paper.

Mary and Me

I find my glasses and see it's a photocopy of an old letter. "Who's it from?"

"It's a letter from my great-grandfather to my grandfather, Henry. I've been going through the old diaries and came across it in one of the earlier ones belonging to my grandfather. He emigrated to New Zealand when he was in his twenties and his father must have posted this to him. Read it. You'll find it very interesting."

The sloping letters are elaborately scripted with large loops and I find it hard to make out the words. It's addressed to Henry and begins with greetings from the family in Hoxton. It acknowledges their receipt of a letter from Henry and tells him that his grandfather passed away on the fifteenth day of October in 1827. It goes on to say no more has been heard of his grandmother, who was plagued with the movement disorder. It finishes by asking him to write with more news of life in the new colony.

"Movement disorder?" I look at Dad. "Do you think this means she had Parkinson's?"

Dad shrugs and slowly shakes his head. "I don't know, but I'm guessing that might be it."

"So what do you think happened to her?"

"I really don't know. It doesn't explain why her death notice isn't in the parish records."

"Now you've really piqued my interest. Have you had any luck finding someone who can search the gravestones?"

"Not as yet."

"Dad, I could ask my friend Liz to look. She's in South London and I'm sure she wouldn't mind."

"I'd appreciate it. It's a mystery that I really want to solve."

"You don't think they did her in, do you? If she was murdered and her body wasn't found then there may not be any record of her death."

He looks at me ruefully. "Not likely."

"Maybe that's why Henry had to leave for New Zealand?"

"He would've been sent to Aussie if he was a convict, not New Zealand," Lauren says.

"But what if he wasn't caught? What if the family shipped him off before the law caught up with him?" Michael asks.

"Don't be silly." Dad looks defensive. "My grandfather wasn't a criminal."

"I'll email Liz after Christmas. I hope she can find something for you. Now, how about we open the presents?"

We have a wonderful family Christmas—swapping presents, much laughter and eating a feast full of rich delicacies. I am so grateful for the support of my family. Without them this journey would be unbearable.

11

Mary, London, 1810

The alms house for impoverished women in Melody Lane has been Mary's home for nigh on three years, ever since she left the family home. It's a home for poor widows, the elderly and those who have found themselves destitute after a life of gin and gambling. Many of these women have given up their miserable life on the streets in exchange for regular food and a dry bed.

Mary tries not to dwell on her previous life and family. However, they are never far from her thoughts and she wonders if John has replaced her with another woman and how the nippers are doing. Many a time she has been tempted to pay them a visit, but she hasn't dared. It wouldn't be hard for them to find her as there aren't many such establishments in the parish, and yet they've never bothered. They are lost to her.

Her limbs are wracked with stiffness and unwanted movements and her body has become slow and stooped. Even the simplest of acts is now difficult and she relies on the good nature of others to help her. Her hair, once golden tresses, is now grey and she no longer has the dexterity or the will to care for it. On rare occasions one of the others will wash and brush it for her. On these days, she feels like a queen.

A gong sounds, calling them to breakfast as she finishes smoothing the blanket over the narrow cot. It is an iron frame raised above the floor with a thin straw mattress that would test the most able of bodies. When she first arrived at the house they had issued her with a straw pillow and two thin blankets. Now she is just thankful for having a bed.

"You coming or what, Mary?" Elizabeth asks, her lined face smiling with genuine affection. Elizabeth has the cot next to Mary and, like many of the women in their dorm, is widowed and left bereft of security and comforts.

"Nearly done." She picks up the crooked walking stick.

The other women have left already by the time Mary struggles her way down the stairs. Elizabeth steadies her with a hand on her elbow. Progress is slow and on entering the dining room they find everyone looking at them expectantly.

The dining room has three long wooden tables with bench seats. Each dormitory has its own table and there are twenty-eight women in each dorm. A large fireplace commands centre position along one wall and high windows line the opposite. Large candelabras hang from the ceiling like one of the great courts of old.

Mary shuffles to an empty seat at the middle table and Elizabeth sits next to her.

Nellie scowls. "Yer took yer time." Her watery, bloodshot eyes betray her propensity for the gin. Liquor and gambling are strictly forbidden in the house and those who dare break the rules are punished, usually with the denial of food and privileges. The gin and endless punishments have done nothing for Nellie's countenance.

Mary chooses not to dignify Nellie's comment with a response and instead bows her head for the grace. It is normal for the women to have to wait for her. It's a frustration she senses daily, especially as breakfast doesn't start until all are seated and only then does Mrs Oldham, their benefactor, say the grace.

They line up in the corner nearest the kitchen for the gruel and two serving girls slop it into their bowls. It's a struggle to hold the bowl steady and by the time she has reached her seat it has spilled. She is not bothered as she no longer has the appetite she once had and the tasteless food is not at all appealing.

She takes a spoonful and just as she raises the spoon to her mouth the shaking worsens and the gruel spills down her bosom.

"Will you look at 'er, drooling like swine in slops!"

A round of sniggers follow.

"Leave her be, you pack of 'arlots!" Elizabeth comes to her rescue. Then she adds in a quiet voice meant only for Mary, "Let me 'elp you."

Thankfully there are some women among them like Elizabeth who are kind and compassionate, without whom this life would be unbearable. Others are uneasy around her and still others continually harass her, showing her nothing but contempt. She wearies of these sharp tongue lashings and finds it best to stay quiet and not draw attention to herself. Their ill humour is driven by fear and, as she also fears whatever it is that has taken control of her movements, she can hardly blame the women.

Elizabeth patiently spoons the gruel into Mary's mouth until the bowl is empty and she swallows it all without a problem. Some days she thinks the thing controlling her has her by the throat and she chokes and splutters, much to the merriment of some of the women.

She doesn't know how long she will be able to stay here. Mrs Oldham, who is deeply religious, considers her possessed and in need of exorcising. Exorcisms are not often spoken of and the mere thought fills Mary with dread, so much so that she has resolved not to be subjected to the treatment. Mrs Oldham says whatever is in her could fly out and inhabit others, as in the Bible story of the possessed man who was rid of his legion of demons only for them to take up residence in a herd of pigs. Mary knows that if she doesn't give in it could jeopardise her place in the home.

Their days here are strictly structured. Those who are able are either sent to work in the kitchen under the supervision of the cook or to the laundry under the supervision of the laundry maid. Their laundry contracts out services to the local middle classes as well as doing the washing for staff and inmates. It is hot physical work and thankfully Mary is deemed unable to work, getting to pass her days sitting in the corner of the dining room. She has become used to her own company and finds comfort in solitude.

*

Mary follows Elizabeth and the other women down the aisle towards the rear of the church where they have just attended morning service. Her legs shake with each step and she is thankful for her stick. It's mandatory for them to attend these services unless they are in the infirmary. Mary attends grudgingly. Even so, Sundays are a day of rest for the workers and have become her favourite days. They always begin with a special breakfast of an extra helping of bread and a pint of beer.

The vicar stands beside the baptismal font and greets the parishioners. He looks Mary over as she approaches and she senses his displeasure. It's likely Mrs Oldham has already talked to him about her condition.

She looks down, ashamed of the stains on her apron from months of spilt food, and mumbles, "Thank you, Father Frederick."

His face is grave as his hand clasps hers in a firm handshake. "God bless you."

She pulls away before he has a chance to say more and steps out through the large oak door and into the sunlight. She stands at the top of the steps, breathes in the warm air and listens to the coo of pigeons in the bell tower above.

Her body totters along the short distance between the church and the alms house where some of the women linger in small groups near the main entrance. With the women having leisure time on Sundays there is always gossip to be heard and much to distract Mary from her plight. But a sword has two edges and it amuses them to hurl cruel taunts at her during their idle time.

As she approaches, Elizabeth and Maud step towards her. Mary stops and leans heavily on her stick.

"We be going out after dinner," Maud says. "Do yer want to join us?" She winds a long lock of her red hair around her finger to make the ringlet curl tighter.

"You'll never find a 'usband if you take 'er along."
Mavis' jibe evokes a chorus of laughter from the others.

"That old 'ag is more likely to cast a spell over 'em."

" 'Old yer scorn!" Elizabeth growls. "Take no 'eed Mary. They've all 'ad a skin full. Best ignore 'em."

"Thank you, but I 'ave me own plans for this afternoon."

She shuffles past them and on towards the entrance, making her way to the dining hall to wait for dinner. Sunday lunch always includes a helping of meat.

The gong sounds and the women hurry in to take their places around the tables. After prayers and dinner many residents queue to seek permission to go out for the afternoon. Rarely does Mary go out these days and then only to wander to the market. On these occasions she often begs for a coin to buy an apple or some fresh bread, a treat after the stale loaves they are dished up by the kitchen. Today she joins the queue.

Mrs Oldham sits behind a table at the front of the queue with a large register open. Worry lines are set deep in her face and a prominent chin flanked by two large jowls perfectly frames her long sharp nose. Her plump figure is clothed with a dark-brown dress edged with cream lace that is topped with a blue apron. Her hair is completely hidden under a generous white cap giving her a foreboding presence. She is a widow with an inheritance who likes it to be known that she is working out her salvation through her charitable works.

Mrs Oldham looks up from the ledger as Mary reaches the front of the queue.

"Ah, Mrs Black." She stares right into Mary's soul with eyes that resemble dark beads.

"Mrs Oldham, may it please yer for me to go out this afternoon?" Mary's voice is little more than a squeak.

Mrs Oldham raises her thick brow. "And for what purpose Mrs Black?"

"To take in the fresh air on such a day as this."

"How could I refuse such a request? But mind you are back in plenty of time for supper." She writes an entry into the ledger. "Next!"

Dismissed, Mary shuffles away. After retrieving her basket from the dormitory she sets out to the familiar cobbled streets. She has been thinking about going on this mission for quite some time. Although not far it takes a mammoth effort and she stops frequently to lean on her stick. Her body is fatigued and the tremors are cruel.

The walk takes her through the marketplace which, despite it being a Sunday, is heaving with sellers and buyers alike. She picks her way through the maze of stalls, taking care not to trip. Boys weave their way through the crowds pushing barrows of produce. The noises warm her heart and stir memories of a life before the troubles.

"Any work for a tinker?" "Flowers for a lady!" "Apples and lemons!" "Chimney sweep! Sweep!" "Meat for sale, fresh from the slaughterhouse!"

Through the melee she hears taunts that she fears are meant for her.

"Look at the old 'ag shakin'!" "Too much gin?" "Shew us yer demons!"

Cringing, with her head bent even lower, she is tempted to turn back and seek the solitude and safety of

Melody Lane, but she is intent on her quest. In a hurry to get away from the market crowd she stumbles and nearly falls on the cobbles, only just catching herself in time. It then takes a minute of resting on her stick before she is ready to walk the last few blocks.

A horse pulling a carriage passes so close that she can almost feel the hair of the beast and she presses into her stick to steady herself. As she nears her destination she stops beside an alleyway and sinks onto a bench seat up against a building, relieved to at last rest her weary limbs. The sound of a hammer tapping metal comes from the smithy's shop on the other side of the alley. The forge is under a veranda in front of the shop and the smithy is bent over an anvil beating the hot metal he holds in a pair of tongs. So intent is he on his workmanship that he doesn't notice her sitting in the shadows. She sucks in a deep breath as she surveys the street.

Opposite is a two-storey brick building that runs the length of the street, its lower level made up of small shop fronts selling a variety of goods from saddles to furniture, boots to clothing and, of course, sweets. Her sweet shop. It is the first time she has dared to come back since that bleak morning nearly three years back. Evenly-spaced sash windows form a neat row along the upper floor. Her eyes come to rest on one of the windows, the one that once was her own bed chamber.

A steady stream of carriages pass by, their horses clip-clopping and the wheels bouncing on the cobbles. People mill about in small groups and some sit in chairs that have been dragged out to the street. Many of them were once her neighbours and she keeps her head down so as not to be recognised. Children run about shouting and playing.

Her heart does a skip as she sees John step out of the shop with Edward close behind. John scans the street. His gaze seems to pause on her before he looks away. It's doubtful he would know her even if she were to enter the shop. Her face has become so gaunt, her hair grey and no longer brushed, her clothes stained and ragged, her figure stooped and her body a bag of bones.

She watches these men of hers as they join a group of neighbours. John stands tall and proud as he holds court, his arms folded across his chest resting on his ample belly. It is a mystery why other men respect him so. Their voices ebb and flow above the hum of street life and she hears the deep resonance of their mirth as it floats on the breeze.

Edward stands tall like his father, looking quite the gentleman in a new-fitting coat over blue breeches and a waistcoat. A cry rings out from a circle of children playing with conkers on the cobbles. Edward steps across to speak with them and she realises they are her own flesh and blood. How they've grown. She chokes back tears at the mere sight of them.

A young girl, in a dress she recalls Mildred wearing when she last saw her, is inconsolable over a conker lying on the ground in front of her. She must be Annie. Her fair ringlets dance about as she laments her lost conker. Beside her Henry, now eight years of age and looking very grown up in a white shirt and breeches the colour of Edward's, speaks with his father. A chubby girl of around six years stands beside him with one hand on her hip and the other dangling a conker on a string. She has long brown ringlets and wears a blue dress that matches the boy's breeches and Mary guesses it is Mildred.

Mary watches her family whose lives have continued without her, until she is blinded by tears. A deep sadness fills her and pierces her heart. Although the sun shines brightly, a dark shadow passes over her and she knows it will stay with her until eternity. She sighs deeply and wipes her tears away with the back of her hand. Then she gets to her feet and shuffles away.

The walk is further than she has been for some time and she is in desperate need of rest, but first she must reach the safety of the alms house. Her steps are barely a stagger and she constantly drags her foot. When she passes back through the marketplace towards Melody Lane she is too tired and dejected to take notice of the taunts, that is, until something hits her shoulder, flicking wet juice across her face. She tries to ignore it by keeping her head down. It's not the first time she has been a target for the amusement of young urchins.

The familiar throng of shrill voices and cackles are a welcome sound once she turns into the lane to the alms house. Men and women mingle on the street in the late afternoon sunshine. One group weaves about with their voices rising above the din and a gin bottle passes between them. Mary is thankful not to attract their attention, for a barb fuelled with the drink can be sharper than a knife.

As she nears the steps her feet freeze as if stuck to the ground while her body continues to move. She teeters forward and falls, hitting the cobbles hard. The walking stick flies free and rolls out of reach.

"Aaie!" Her voice is barely a scream. The pain pierces her head and tired body. Tears well up and overflow.

Peals of laughter ring out.

Elizabeth and Maud come to her side.

"You be all right?" Elizabeth asks.

Maud looks stricken. "Yer bleedin'!"

Mary touches her forehead and feels the blood that runs down her temple.

"Let us 'elp you to the infirmary." Elizabeth offers her hand.

Mary is too upset to speak. They help her inside to the dorm room used to treat the sick, where they lay her on a bed. The nurse treats the wounds, but it is Mary's heart that is broken and there is neither a bandage nor salve that can mend it.

12

Rose, Hauraki Gulf, January 2020

It's been over three years since those two words were spoken over me. The first year was a rollercoaster of a ride as we adjusted to our new normal. Finding the right dosages for the cocktail of drugs has required lots of experimentation, with each change in dosage made at a painstakingly slow rate to avoid any nasty side effects. I've had to deal with low blood pressure and other changes as I worked to find the right blend my body could tolerate. It's a fine balance and when I noticed some dyskinesia in my little finger, signalling too much Levodopa, I reduced the meds slightly to find the optimal dosage, for now.

The sun shines on the Hauraki Gulf and a breeze lifts the surface water into patterns of small ripples. I watch as a light squall moves across the water towards us, filling the sail and tickling my bare skin as it passes us by in its wake. I stand at *Sano Diyo*'s helm surveying the surrounding sea. We are heading for Aotea Island.

Splashes in the distance break the expansive blue and I point towards the horizon. "Dolphins! Three o'clock."

"Let's tack around." Gary leaps to his feet.

"You take the helm. I want to haul on the ropes."

"Are you sure?"

"It's my workout."

Gary relieves me of my position at the helm. "Prepare to tack!"

I take the genoa sheet out of its cleat and brace myself. "Ready."

"Stand by." He points the nose through the wind and adds, "Tacking."

The sails flap as the wind crosses the bow and *Sano Diyo* comes around. I bend my knees slightly, straighten my back and breathe steadily as I haul on the starboard sheet. Hand over hand I haul it in, feeling a new strength in my arms. Then I crank in the genoa sail tight with the winch and tidy the ropes.

"Good effort." He pauses before adding, "A year ago you couldn't have hauled on the sheet like that."

His words are encouraging and I bask in them. "Yeah, I feel so much better. Look at this." I clench my fists and hold them up, making my skinny arms show off their biceps.

He laughs.

"Hey, don't be so rude. They're actually growing." I then hold out my arms, hands flat with fingers spread. "And look at this, no tremor."

"That's amazing. You look more flexible when you move too."

"I am. I barely notice the rigidity."

"It's obvious in your movements. You are more agile than I've seen you for years."

The water makes a gentle swooshing sound on the hull as we head towards the dolphins who now swim towards us. I hurry down the companionway to get my camera. I have so many photos of dolphins, but I can't resist taking more in the hope of getting the perfect nature shot.

I navigate my way to the bow with camera at the ready, feeling sure-footed despite the motion of the water. Several large bottlenose dolphins are riding the bow wave and I sit down, my legs dangling over the side, almost close enough to touch them. It's a large pod and dolphins swim around and under us. One swims alongside and we eye each other with mutual curiosity. I never tire of watching these beautiful creatures of the sea. They seem so free and so playful. If I had to live in the sea I'd want to be one of these.

"Let Ray take over and come and join me," I shout, using our affectionate name for the autohelm. More photos. I'm in my happy place, loving life despite the Parkinson's diagnosis. There's so much to live for.

Gary, now sitting beside me, asks, "Aren't they amazing?"

A large dolphin leaps high out of the water. "Why is it that when I'm looking through the viewfinder they're always quiet and as soon as I take my eye from the camera they show off?"

"You'll have to ask 'Murphy' about that one."

The dolphins soon lose interest and as suddenly as they appeared they swim off, perhaps answering the call to join some distant mission.

"It's so hard to get the perfect shot." I switch off the camera.

We sit, feet dangling, content with the world around us. The sea moves continuously, its gentle motion producing slight swells that occasionally break with a small amount of white foam. The breeze is consistent, perfect for sailing. The land ahead, Aotea Island, is still faint on the horizon and Kawau Island behind us appears equally distant. Gannets circle overhead and catapult themselves like thunderbolts, beak first into the sea.

"You're different, in a good way. Are you aware of the change in you?" Gary asks.

"I think so. I do feel stronger."

"That's part of it. You also seem more resilient, even more independent and definitely more adventurous." He lies back on the deck, soaking in the sunshine. "You've always been happy to take the helm and let me do most of the rope work, even before your diagnosis, but that's changing."

I lie back beside him, feeling the slight vibration of water through the hull. "I am more confident in my own strength and that's simply due to my workouts. It's because I'm more aware of not allowing myself to be rescued that I want to do more for myself. I'm scared that one day I might be completely dependent and I don't want that."

"Looking back, even before your diagnosis, I think you had lost a lot of your confidence. Now you seem to have more than regained it."

"It's funny that one of the positives from having Parkinson's is that it's given me more determination to try things myself and to not let you do them for me. Before I let you do stuff because you are stronger than me, no question. Now I just want to achieve physical things myself." I pause and scan the horizon, then add more quietly, "While I can."

"Let's not have any of that negative talk." He looks at me and pauses. "You promised me."

"You're right though. I am changing and I think it's a positive change. I'm much more aware that I can't let you rescue me, that I need to do things myself. Even simple things, like driving. How many times do you automatically get in behind the wheel when we are going somewhere? I need to do more of that myself."

"Is that why you were so keen to put your name down for Outward Bound?"

"I guess so. I want to prove to myself that I can overcome my fears and I want to achieve new physical goals, while I'm still able."

A throbbing noise sounds in the distance and I sit up to see a launch coming towards us, its motor disturbing the tranquillity of the ocean. I watch it pass, cutting a path through the sparkling aqua water, leaving a trail of white foam behind to fan out across the gentle rise and fall of the sea.

"These three years since your diagnosis have gone past so fast. It's been a difficult ride, but I like where you've got to."

"Our lives seem to have settled into a pattern and I admit it's way better than I'd originally expected."

"You work hard at keeping as well as you can, all credit to you. You could just give up. Your fitness regime takes a lot of work."

"There is no choice. I keep thinking I'm on this rat wheel and I just can't afford to get off it."

Gary sits up with his cap now lopsided and looks at me. "Maybe you should think of it as something a little more positive than a rat wheel. A rat wheel suggests futility and you're living proof that your efforts have been worthwhile. Rather than a rat wheel, I'd call it swimming against a rip, and you're winning."

"I like that. Getting closer to the shore and safety is like getting closer to the cure."

"Exactly. Athletes train for events. They set themselves goals. Without goals it would be more difficult to keep the disciplined training up. What's your number one goal?"

I answer without hesitation, "To stay well until the cure."

"That's a good goal to have. It might be useful to set some shorter term goals, like events. Maybe some fun runs or something like that."

"I miss my squash, but I don't want to go through all the injuries again. I do get what you mean about being more positive."

"Maybe you should think of your exercise regime as part of your way of life, like going to work each day, and less of a rat wheel as that implies drudgery."

"Like breathing," I reply. "It has to be done and without it where would we be?"

He grins. "For starters, we wouldn't be out here enjoying this paradise."

We sit in comfortable silence for a while, lost in thought.

"How about I check our position and make us some lunch." I carefully get to my feet.

"Sounds good. Although there's no hurry." He settles back down on the deck and pulls his cap over his face to shield it from the sun.

A faint honking noise draws my attention back to the water in time to see a little blue penguin glide past. When it spots us it dives under the surface.

I head to the helm and note our progress on the GPS. The second half of the passage goes as smoothly as the first and in less than six hours we are anchoring just out from the island to fish. In no time at all we have fresh snapper for our dinner. We weigh anchor and motor the short distance to our destination. Cliffs rise steeply from the water on our port side as we navigate our way around rocks the size of small islands. We pass the submerged Passage Rock and then a mussel farm. We head for Man O' War Passage, a narrow stretch of water between two walls of rock marking the harbour entrance. Once through the passage we are met with the expanse of water and inlets that is Fitzroy Harbour, one of our favourite places.

A south-easterly breeze is forecast and we choose to spend the night in Kaiaraara Inlet. Several vessels are already moored in the bay and we choose a spot to drop anchor not too far from the entrance to the walking track.

After a quick bathe in the cool water we prepare to settle in for the night and are soon sitting in the boat's cockpit, with snacks and drinks. The bay is sheltered from the breeze and the water is mirror-like. Our dinghy floats lazily on the end of the painter tied to our stern. Bush-laden hills are reflected in the deep blue water. It is so peaceful. You can hear the call of the kaka, the song of the tui and korimako in the bush, the squawk of the sea birds as they

Mary and Me

fly over and around us and the occasional plop as one hits the water. A pateke duck comes over to check us out and pleads for us to throw it some food. It hops up onto our dinghy to keep vigil. A kahawai breaks the surface. Our world is at peace.

*

I wake to a gentle rocking motion and stretch, remembering where I am. I hear the distant whine of a motor and know that its wake has reached us. Gary stirs beside me.

"Fancy starting the day with a swim?" I ask.

"Sure. What do you want to do today?"

"We could walk up to the old kauri dam."

It's a good track and a decent climb with lots of steps, but the view and the bush make it spectacular and well worth the effort.

"Great idea. Do you want to get some paddle boarding in first?" he asks.

The paddle board was his Christmas present to me and I'm still mastering it. The idea behind it is to expand my exercise regimes while on the boat with the intention of improving my core strength and balance.

"I guess so. I may need to pace myself as I don't want to get too tired."

"You can do it." He pulls himself out of our bunk. "C'mon, I'll race you into the water."

Before I can change into my bikini I hear a splash and know I'm beaten. I dive in after him and swim around *Sano Diyo* a couple of times. The water is refreshing and I love the invigorating feeling it gives me. We get out and drip dry in the early morning sunshine. It's the perfect way to start the day.

Breakfast is a delicious omelette filled with spinach and feta. We sit in the cockpit to devour it before washing it down with a mug of good coffee. I attempt to challenge my brain with a crossword, but the beauty of my surroundings is a welcome distraction. The bay is idyllic with the water still like glass. At the top of the bay the depth tapers out into mud flats littered with debris washed down the river from the forest in countless storms. Tall peaks cloaked in bush rise above the valley to form the skyline.

Gary stirs from his prostrate position along the portside cockpit seat. "I didn't tell you about my chat with Tricia last week."

"No, how did it go?" I ask.

"She said a few things that really bothered me, surprising really."

I lie down along the starboard seat to soak in the sun's rays. "What do you mean?"

"She's struggling to cope with Eric and wasn't overly sympathetic to his symptoms. She said she didn't sign on to be his caregiver and spoke like he's a burden."

"That's awful. How's he doing?"

"Not so good. It sounds like he's struggling with depression. He's not active like you and he's not fighting it. She's focused on how it's changed her life and I'd say their relationship is under pressure."

"How can we help?"

"Probably by just being there for them and being available if either one of them needs to talk. I made the offer to Tricia on behalf of us both."

Mary and Me

"Good, but that's sad. They were always such a tight couple."

"You can't predict how others will react to something as life changing as Parkinson's. It puts huge stress on them, their family dynamics and their futures. It can be a tough sentence, especially if you lose respect for someone because of the way they're handling it."

"Is that what you think happened to Tricia?"

"I think so. She came across as not being in a good place and we'll need to support them in any way we can. Maybe it was just a bad day and she needed to unload. Parkinson's disease isn't for the weak. It takes a lot of courage."

"It makes me appreciate you even more. Although you look at me with rose-tinted glasses you're good at encouraging me, especially when I'm finding things tough going. I need that."

"My lenses aren't rose-tinted. I simply see you as you are."

"Maybe or maybe not, but I'm okay with it. I certainly need your support to keep focused on the fight."

"I admit that I've been afraid of the worst-case scenario that has hung over us like a brooding cloud. But now, after seeing how you are dealing with it, that cloud has retreated. It's still there, it's on the distant horizon but it isn't nearly as dark and ominous. Thankfully your bad days have become a rarity."

"I intend to keep it that way."

Slight splashing sounds come from near the boat and a school of small silvery fish break the surface, panicked and desperate to flee from unknown predators. Gary leaps to his feet and grabs his fishing rod from its holder before attaching a silver lure.

"Fancy a kingfish?" He casts it overboard and it plops close to the fish.

He winds it in and repeats the process, but the fish have already turned away and are heading back out of the bay. Their presence hasn't been lost on the gannets who now circle overhead and dive for their breakfast.

"Those poor little fish. What a miserable life. They're hunted from below and above at the same time. They really don't stand a chance." I stand and stretch lazily, "I'm going to take the paddle board around the bay."

I climb down to the transom and untie my new toy. Taking the paddle in one hand I gingerly step first one foot and then the other onto the board, taking care to keep my weight central so as not to lose my balance. I stand with knees slightly bent and begin to paddle. The board is pumped full of air and moves easily across the water. I navigate my way around the dozen boats still sitting at anchor and head for the mussel beds at the entrance to the bay.

A launch pulls up its anchor and its motor whines as it speeds out of the bay, its wake rippling across the water. I brace myself and turn to meet the wake head on. Although I'm more confident paddling than I was at Christmas time, my balance is still challenged and my left side starts to shake, reacting to the stress. *I can do this.* The board floats over the first wave and then the subsequent waves. I remain standing. I turn the board and complete a full circle and then another circle in the opposite direction. My balance has improved so much even though it's been only a few weeks since I first started using the board. Then I could

Mary and Me

barely stand up, let alone paddle standing. I complete my circumnavigation of the bay and return to *Sano Diyo*.

Gary is in the cockpit watching. "Looking good!"

"I'm getting better." I come alongside and step onto the transom. "I feel much more confident."

"You look it."

After a snack and a drink we get ready for the long trek up to the kauri dam. Rather than put the outboard on the dinghy Gary has set up the oars. I pass him the backpack, camera gear and shoes and step into the inflatable. He's already sitting in the rower's seat.

"I'll row," I say.

"Are you sure?" he asks. Up until recently he would always row for me.

"Absolutely. It's my workout."

We shift around and I take up the oars. I steer a straight line for the small beach at the start of the walking track.

"You've definitely changed."

"Use it or lose it."

"I'm proud of you."

"No need to be. I'm just trying to future-proof."

We reach the shallows, hop out and drag the dinghy up to above the high tide mark.

The walking track ascends steeply up the hillside before levelling out and following the contour of the bay towards the river valley. The sun lights up the fronds of tree ferns providing a lime green glow in contrast to their dark trunks and the dirt path covered in dry leaf litter. Smaller ferns compete for the dappled light under the tree ferns.

Snatches of sparkling water are just visible through the fernery.

I lead and set a brisk walking pace, knowing Gary will have no problem keeping up. We don't talk much, for we love to listen to the sounds of the bush. We get to the first bridge and use the disinfectant provided for our footwear, keen to prevent the spread of the kauri die-back disease. A little further on we come to the clearing where a DOC hut sits beside the river.

Across the clearing we climb the few steps leading up to a swing bridge that spans the river. The bridge dazzles brightly in the sunlight, its wire mesh leading to the bush beyond. We sway our way across it, only stopping at the other side to take a photo. We walk on and up, roughly following the river valley through groves of kanuka, nikau palms, tawa, kohekohe and others. Young kauri are attempting to reclaim their forest while mature kauri are noticeably absent.

The forest is alive with birdsong. Every now and then I stop to photograph a bird or a stump sculpture or bush fungi or an impressive cobweb glistening in the sunlight, spun with the mastery of nature. We cross bridges over tributaries, step around landslides and climb many steps. It's a hot day and the walk is challenging, but I'm in my element.

Eventually we arrive at the old kauri dam lookout. The kauri dam was built in 1909 to accommodate the giant kauri that once dominated the bush. These ancient trees were greatly valued, providing hard straight timber for ship building, among other uses. Such was man's greed that the forest was plundered until barely a kauri was left standing. When the dam was full of the logs the timber gates would be opened and the kauri logs would race down the river scouring out everything in their path until they reached the bay. From there they were taken to market.

A few years ago this feat of bush engineering was intact but a storm in 2016 virtually wiped it out. Now all that is left of it are two great kauri logs at its base. The timber gates were smashed and spewed down the river during the storm.

Large boulders, pocked with crater-like holes resembling Swiss cheese, form the riverbed that flows steeply down to the bay below. Towering above the dam are huge, rocky pinnacles half-clothed with bush, their sheer cliff faces rising vertically to the sky. It's an impressive vista, a worthy place to sit and have our lunch.

The return trip always seems to go faster and we soon make our way back to *Sano Diyo*, better for the time spent soaking up the bush.

That evening we sit in the cockpit having our usual pre-dinner snacks and drinks.

"I've just realised I didn't give a thought to Parkinson's the entire bushwalk apart from when I popped my tablets. That's a first in a very long time." I fiddle with a sail tie.

"Why do you think that was?" Gary asks.

"I was content and my rigidity was barely noticeable as was the tremor. They're normally a constant reminder. I guess I was distracted by the peace and beauty of the bush."

"You are a lot better. I really mean that. I hardly notice you've got it. And I love that you are sticking to your exercise regime as well as constantly challenging yourself with new things."

"I guess I'm lucky I'm able to do all these things."

The sun is already low on the horizon, coating everything with a golden glow. The wispy clouds are turning a faint tinge of pink and the pastel shades are reflected in the tranquil bay. I am so blessed to be here, in this moment.

In the early days I avoided Parkinson's organised events and discussion groups because I didn't want to be reminded of what my future might look like when seeing others struggling through later stages. Having come to terms with my illness and having greater confidence in my ability to fight it I've been getting more involved in the Parkinson's organisation. Through this work I've met new friends with Parkinson's who are truly inspirational. For some the disease is more advanced and I admire their positive attitude and their bravery.

"I've been thinking I want to use my Parkinson's for good. I've tried to focus on the positives and that's helped me cope. Now I'd like to use my experience to help others. It's a bit like turning a traumatic event into something good."

"You're already doing voluntary work for Parkinson's."

"That's using the skills I've developed through my work. What I'm talking about is helping more people, especially early-onset or those early in their journey, to deal with Parkinson's. I think there are a lot of people like me who are trying to face it alone and don't want to be confronted with what might lie ahead through seeing others further along in their Parkinson's journey. They need to realise it's worth fighting and to be given hope."

"Do you think you would've benefited from hearing how others were fighting it early on after your diagnosis?"

"Definitely. I would have been encouraged if I saw them living well and positively. I still am."

"And if they weren't?"

"To be honest, back then I would've been somewhat discouraged. I needed to see people doing well." I reach for a handful of nuts and an olive from the plate of goodies. "Arguably the worst of the symptoms is not so much the movement disorders but rather the apathy, loss of confidence, even anxiety and depression. It's these symptoms that prevent people from working and enjoying life at least as much as the motor symptoms. It's a vicious cycle as they contribute to stress and a lack of energy, making exercise even more difficult and the movement disorder worse."

"There must be a lot of people out there trying to get through their diagnosis and not yet wanting to encounter other people with Parkinson's for fear of having to confront their own potentially miserable future." Gary looks thoughtful.

"I'm sure it's a very natural response. I hate to think of people being blindsided by the apathy and missing out on living a fuller life." I gaze out over the water. "Do you recall Lauren talking about her netball friend who has been diagnosed with young-onset Parkinson's?"

"Jasmine, wasn't it?"

"Yes. I think I'll suggest to Lauren that she sets up a meeting. Maybe I can help by passing on some of the positive things that I've learned." I watch the gannets dive into the bay.

"Maintaining a positive attitude is a real asset and you've certainly found a formula of exercise and diet that works for you."

"Having a supportive family really helps. Not everyone is this lucky. And let's not forget the drugs. They do help even if the doc called it a homeopathic dose." I help myself to another olive and chase it down with a sip of the crisp cold wine. "It's been a great day and I'm so thankful to be here."

"There'll be many more great days. Parkinson's has stolen enough of them already. Time to take some back."

"*So, take that Parkinson's!*" I raise my glass in a mock toast.

*

The rest of the holiday passes in a blur of leisure activities, filled with reading and sunbathing, sailing, swimming, fishing, trekking and general boating activities. Living with a degenerative disease makes this time even more precious and we relish every moment.

I return home with renewed vigour, determined to make the most of every day and, more than ever, I want to push myself to my physical limits to stay as fit and healthy as I can, at least until a cure is found.

13

Rose, Auckland, March 2020

I'm sitting outside a café in the CBD when I spot Lauren and her friend in the distance. Lauren's trademark long blonde hair is tied up in a ponytail that bounces from side to side as they hurry towards me. The young woman with her is tall and athletic like Lauren, with short black hair. They both wear shorts and T-shirts. Lauren breaks into a grin and hurries towards me.

"Sorry we're late." She hugs me and moves her sunglasses to the top of her head. "It was hard finding a carpark. Mum, meet Jasmine, my friend from netball."

"Lauren says she's told you I've just been diagnosed with young-onset Parkinson's." Jasmine takes the seat opposite me.

"Yes, she mentioned that. When were you diagnosed?"

"Just three months ago. It's been a bit of a shock as I'm only thirty-five." Jasmine looks down and fiddles with her rings.

"I'm really sorry to hear that. How are you coping with it?"

Her brows change her pretty face into a frown. "It's hard. My greatest fear is that I won't be there for my girls as they grow up."

"How old are they?"

"Grace is nine and Cindy is seven years old. They're too young to understand what's going on with me." She turns her head slightly to gaze out the window. "I'm worried about how long I'll be able to work as we have a mortgage and need my income. It's so hard to juggle family, domestics, work and sport."

"It's tough when you get it so young. I'm part of an online Parkinson's community and am surprised at how many young people are diagnosed with it. The youngest I've heard of is only twelve. I don't know if more people are getting it younger or if we're just hearing of more. Did you know it's the fastest growing neurological disease? Some are calling it a man-made pandemic."

"Why's that?"

"They say toxins in the environment are largely to blame for the increase."

"I hadn't heard that. I hope you don't mind telling me about your journey. Lauren says you're doing really well and have even reduced your drugs."

"That's right, I've dropped them twice now. I don't have all the answers, but I'm happy to answer any questions and to share what I've found helps me. People with Parkinson's all seem to react differently to the disease. Maybe some of the things that have helped me will also help you."

"Have you ordered yet?" Lauren asks.

"No, I wanted to wait for you."

We go to the cabinet and study the food. The array of tasty looking treats is tempting. However, I play it safe and choose a salad.

Lauren turns to me. "Still off the sugar?"

"Yep, I think it helps so I'm sticking with it. My body is now used to not having the added sugar and the craving's gone. In fact, most sweet things taste too sweet now and I actually prefer savoury."

We order our food and drinks and move to a table near the street.

I turn to Jasmine. "Tell me about your work. What is it you do?"

"I work in a microbiology lab. I love my work but am worried about the future and how Parkinson's will affect it. I haven't told anyone at work yet—I don't know how." Her eyes are glassy as if she's trying to hold back tears. "I'm scared it'll be misunderstood and be seen as a liability."

"What's your boss like?"

"He's okay, not really the compassionate type." This time the tears overflow and she pulls a tissue out of her bag and wipes them with a shaky hand. "I've been trying to hide my symptoms."

"Do your symptoms interfere with your work?"

"Sometimes. On a bad day I find I'm having to do things more slowly."

"Are there some tasks that you find you can still do easily despite the symptoms?"

She hesitates for a long moment. "There are some things that're okay."

"Why don't you consider approaching your boss and letting him know what you're dealing with? Maybe suggest changing your responsibilities so that you do more of the things you can easily do and fewer of the ones that have become difficult. Do you think he'd be supportive if you take the initiative on this?"

"Possibly. I'm scared about losing my job as we really need the money for the mortgage and it could be hard finding another job with Parkinson's."

"I can understand that. How's your husband coping?"

"He struggles with it. I think he's as scared as I am. He doesn't like talking about it."

I nod slowly while considering how much harder it must be to receive this life sentence as a young mum. "I'm sure my husband would be willing to talk to him if you think it would help."

The waitress brings our food and we eat in silence for a while.

"I've told Jasmine a little about how you're fighting Parkinson's with diet and exercise," Lauren says.

"I'm interested in hearing more." Jasmine's eyes are no longer wet.

"What seems to work for me is a combination of good diet and gut health, and my exercise regime, along with the drugs. In a letter to my GP my neurologist put the improvement in my motor symptoms down to my regular and varied exercise programme. I've also read of many other people with Parkinson's getting similar benefits from exercise. It really does work."

"That's awesome." Jasmine looks impressed. "What sort of exercise?"

"I try and mix cardio with strength training, balance and new routines that my body has no memory of. And I try to throw in some multi-tasking with the repetitive exercises to really challenge my brain. It takes a lot of time, but it's worth the discipline to keep going."

Jasmine looks downcast. "Time is something I don't have much of and it sounds expensive."

"I'm doing it on the cheap. To get the variation by joining different classes would be too expensive. I use YouTube and enjoy different types of dance routines."

"What sort of routines?" Jasmine asks.

"I started doing exercises designed especially for Parkinson's, but they were too easy for the stage I'm at. Now I try routines based on ballet, hip hop, African dance, Latin dance, kickboxing, Pilates and the list goes on. It must be hilarious to watch because I'm not very coordinated although I am getting better. I heard a talk by a physio who said if you can only do about fifty per cent then it's probably the right level for you. So I figure I've got it about right. I mix these with cardio exercises."

"Why fifty per cent?" Lauren asks. "That's not even a pass in my book."

"For neuroplasticity, a process where you develop new connections, it seems to require your brain to be continually challenged with new and complex movements."

"What about pole dancing?" Lauren laughs.

I laugh with her. "Not before Dad installs the pole. I've thought about belly dancing though."

"That I have to see!"

Jasmine joins in with the laughter and it's good to see her more relaxed.

I hold up my wrist showing my Polar watch. "This is awesome. I'm printing out my monthly graphs of exercise and heart rate zones. I admit I'm such a nerd that I can't bear having gaps on the charts and so it helps motivate me to get out and exercise daily. One of the best prezzies ever, perfect for a Parkie."

"What about the keto diet? Will you go back on it?" Lauren asks.

"Do you know about keto?" I ask Jasmine.

She nods the affirmative. "High performance athletes use it."

"I'm sure the diet contributed to my overall well-being and my energy levels." I stop to chew on a forkful of my salad then tell Jasmine about my experience with keto and the lasting effects.

"Maybe I'll give keto a go," Jasmine says.

I smile and look at her. "We're lucky to have an early diagnosis when we're still fit and able to have intensive workouts. I think my diet has helped normalise my gut health. It has helped me to sleep through the night and, in turn, I have energy and seem to be keeping a lid on the lethargy and feelings of apathy. This has helped me push my fitness and I'm now stronger and have better balance as a result. I even have muscles where I thought they were lost for good. I think the fitness has helped with the tremor. And feeling better about my tremor has helped me regain my confidence."

"Mum's even paddleboarding." Lauren looks at me with pride.

"I'm thinking of entering the Round the Bays as a runner and to raise funds for Parkinson's. Why don't you join me?" I look from Lauren to Jasmine.

Lauren raises an eyebrow. "Parkinson's really has changed you."

"Yup, and in ways you couldn't even imagine. I've discovered new superpowers."

They laugh with me.

"The race is a great idea. I'll enter and run with you," Lauren says.

"You'll be way out in front. Just because I have new superpowers doesn't mean I'll be any good. I'm no runner and never have been, but I want to give it a go. This will be my first ever race and I don't even know how far it is."

"It's 8.4 km." Lauren sits back and grins. "I think you should do it and we'll definitely be part of the support team."

The girls look reflective as we sip our coffee.

Jasmine puts her cup down and eyes me, her expression serious. "How do you stay positive?"

"It's not always easy as dopamine is a reward chemical in the brain, but it's important. It would be too easy to focus on the negatives and let fear drag me down, which could rapidly turn into a downward spiral. One of the hard things about Parkinson's is the symptoms are always there, serving as a reminder of the disease, and it can be all-consuming. I try to focus on living in the moment and making the best of my life. The disease may be outside my control, but my attitude is something I can control. I try to stay focused on the positives."

"What do you see as the positives?" Jasmine asks.

"For starters it could be a lot worse. I'm still here after all." I smile and add, "I'm able to have time with my family. I'm not in constant pain. I've met and made some wonderful new friends through Parkinson's. I have a new purpose in trying to beat this thing. I've learned to live one day at a time and to enjoy life more. And to top it off, this is the best time to have Parkinson's because there's so much research going on that I'm sure the cure will come in my lifetime. These are just off the top of my head. I'm sure I could come up with more if I put my mind to it."

"You should write them up and post them somewhere you can see them, especially if you are feeling a bit low," Lauren says, always the pragmatist.

"Great idea." I stare at my lovely daughter and am filled with warmth.

Jasmine sighs. "It's such a complex disease that I find it all a bit daunting."

"Be encouraged as there's a lot of reason for hope right now. I follow a website each month that summarises nearly one thousand articles of the scientific research relating to Parkinson's. So many studies and some are looking quite hopeful. I believe there will be a breakthrough in my lifetime and my goal is to stay as well as I can until that discovery, through prayer, exercise, positive thinking, pills and diet. I call it staying PEPPD. I have to believe they'll find a way to stop the progression of the disease in my lifetime."

Jasmine picks up her phone. "Can you give me the acronym again? I want to make a note of it."

"PEPPD—prayer, exercise, positive thinking, pills and diet."

We spend the remainder of our time talking about kids and sport. As we are leaving Lauren promises me that the first thing she's going to do when she gets home will be to fill out the entry for the Round the Bays race.

*

The doorbell rings and I run down the stairs and open it to find my dad leaning on the doorjamb, removing his shoes.

"Come on up. You're just in time for coffee." I give him a hug.

"I could do with a coffee. I've had to fight the traffic in town. I swear it's getting worse."

We climb the stairs and I go into the kitchen and make our coffees.

"Did you get the email I forwarded from Liz? She's put some real effort into finding those gravestones," I say.

"Yes, and she's been a great help although we're no further on with solving the mystery." He pulls some paper out of his pocket and unfolds it. "I've printed the photos of the inscriptions. Mary is named as John's wife on his gravestone, but it doesn't say she also is laid to rest there."

"Liz said in her email that she went to all the old graveyards in the vicinity of Hoxton and didn't find her gravestone anywhere."

"There's no doubt that the ones she found are our ancestors. The dates are correct. It's a mystery all right. Why wouldn't she be buried nearby?"

"I imagine divorce was rare in those days."

"I think so." He sighs. "And if they were divorced she wouldn't be listed as his wife on his headstone. There must be a record of her somewhere. She can't just disappear."

"Given the letter you found suggests she may have had Parkinson's, could she have been put in a sanatorium or some sort of home for the sick?"

"It's possible. It'd have to be nearby because they didn't travel far back then and you'd think she'd still be buried with the family. It's so frustrating not to know what happened to her."

"Keep digging Dad. Something will turn up." I hand him a mug of steaming coffee.

We go outside to enjoy the sunshine, and under the shade of the umbrella we solve the world's problems while watching butterflies and bees flitting about the garden, content in each other's company. It's good to be alive.

*

I start my running training the very next day. Gary, a keen runner, is my number one encourager and I need him to keep me at it, especially in those times of apathy. I start small, running the length of our street and back. It's just 1.8 km. I keep mixing the exercise routines with the running and find it's a good start to my days. And every time I extend my distance it's a new milestone. And I think, *Take that Parkinson's!*

"You are running much better," Gary says one morning. "You're looking more effortless, striding out better and your posture is good. Your left leg is still dragging a bit so try to focus on lifting it a little higher. Try to focus also on swinging your left arm. Good work though. I reckon you could be a reasonable runner."

"That's funny 'cos all my life I've avoided running for the sake of running. Give me a ball to chase any day."

"How about we run five kilometres?"

And we do. It takes some real grit as the final hill home is a killer, but I make it and I'm elated.

"Good effort," Gary says, as we stretch to warm down.

"Did you know that intense exercise apparently has a neuroprotective effect?" I ask. "I've been reading about it through Doctor Google."

"It's got to be good for your balance, your agility and mobility as well as your energy levels and general well-being."

"It is and it's thought to modulate the dopamine system as well as protect dopamine neurons against toxic assaults. In other words, it could slow down the disease and even improve the symptoms. I think this is based on animal studies, but it gives credibility to what I seem to be experiencing."

"You can't lose then," says my ever-positive husband.

"Right now I feel so good that I figure I've just manufactured a heap of dopamine. My substantia nigra must be doing something. I definitely feel rewarded."

"It's only two weeks to the run and you're on target to run the course without walking."

"I'm determined to run it all and not to let my sponsors down," I say.

I am committed to my goal. When I entered the race I opted to link my entry to a fundraiser for Parkinson's New Zealand. Friends and family have been donating to the cause via Facebook, without me doing anything other than paying my entry fee.

"What's the tally up to?" he asks.

"Fifteen hundred, give or take a little. I never expected to raise this sort of money for Parkinson's. It's easy fundraising and all I have to do is run the race."

"How're the feet?"

I'd recently been diagnosed with osteoarthritis in my joints and my feet hurt when flexing them, walking or running, especially up hill.

"Aching. I just have to keep them going."

"Embrace your pain, Grasshopper!"

"Easy for you to say. Sometimes I feel like it's two steps forward and one step back."

"Then you're definitely winning. Roll on the race."

*

I keep up the training and the day of the race dawns. We get up early and drive into the city centre to find a park near the start line. It's a stunning day. The harbour sparkles under a sunny and windless sky. These days I'm more susceptible to temperature extremes and I worry the heat may get to me and I might fail to achieve my goal. To help calm the nerves we stop at a café near the waterfront and chill with good coffee until it's time to meet the others.

As we near the start line on Quay St the hordes become a massive seething crowd of 34,000 runners and walkers. Many are in fancy dress or branded with their particular cause. We walk past the port, past rows of portaloos and find a spot at the front of the joggers. There's a carnival atmosphere with loudspeakers blaring, screens showing some of the more out-there costumes as well as interviews with Radio DJs and sport celebrities advocating fitness and wellness. My nerves spur on my Parkie bladder and I find myself in the long queue for the portaloos not once but twice. People of all ages, shapes and ethnicities mingle and bibs showing the race numbers bind us together in a common cause. The crowd is buoyant, buzzing with excited expectation.

A crane makes a good landmark where we wait for the others. Michael and partner Ali find us in time to join in a warm-up routine led by a fitness advocate on the large screen. As the big digital clocks count down to the start of the race the tension mounts before the hooter sounds and we're off.

With such a dense crowd we start slowly and pick our way around joggers and walkers, carefully avoiding entanglement with limbs and small bodies. It's chaotic, with lots of laughter and light-hearted banter. We pass runners and walkers of all ages and abilities, spidermen and caped superheroes with their undies on the outside, buzzy bees and butterflies, teddy bears and pandas, ballerinas and clowns, children in pushchairs and people in wheelchairs. Teams representing a myriad of charities and businesses are identified by their matching T-shirts.

I fall into the rhythm that has become my running mantra—slow deep breathing while focusing on shoulders back, tummy in and lifting my feet. I'm determined I won't adopt the typical stooped Parkinson's posture and I try to use every opportunity to maintain my core strength.

We follow the road around the Waitemata Harbour that gives a stunning backdrop, past drink stations and onlookers who cheer us on. Gary runs at my side constantly encouraging me. Lauren is no doubt way out in front with the good runners. Musicians accompany us. The vibe is upbeat. Michael and Ali are in party mode and I envy their youth and the fact they can run without training. Street entertainers mingle with the contestants. Michael and Ali dance around them high-fiving and generally having a good time. I don't chat. I have no excess energy in this heat, but stay focused on running to the finish line, breathing in and out, in and out.

As I round another corner into yet another bay, St Heliers Bay and the finish line come into view. I can do this. Spurred on by the crowd I dig in and sprint across the finish line. Adrenaline pumps through my veins as I clock up another milestone—my first race and my first time running 8.4 km.

"Congratulations!" Gary pulls me into a sweaty bear hug. "You didn't just do it. You nailed it."

"You smashed it!" Michael gives me a hug. "How do you feel?"

"Absolutely elated. I was worried I wouldn't be able to run it all in this heat—but I did it."

Ali hugs me. "Congratulations!"

"Where on earth do you get all your energy? With all your fooling around you and Michael must have run twice the distance I did."

"That was such a fun race. Let's do it again next year." Her words are coated with a strong Irish accent.

"And you thought your mother wasn't a runner." Gary looks at Michael.

"Mum, you're not such a bad runner after all," Michael says.

"A year ago I couldn't have done this. Five years ago I wouldn't have tried. I think I'm getting better with age."

"Like a fine wine." Gary eyes me with pride.

I glow in my success. Our prize for crossing the finish line is a bottle of Pump water and a shiny medal.

The water goes down a treat and my medal takes pride of place around my neck.

Lauren and Jasmine find us. They'd met up at the start of the race and they ran it together in a good time, well ahead of us. We all swap stories of the race before taking the obligatory selfie.

Someone touches me on the shoulder.

"Rose, I didn't expect to see you here." Fran beams at me, looking young and fit in her running gear with her medal dangling proudly over her top.

"Hey, Fran, Brian." I hug her and add, "Good to see you."

I haven't seen Brian since the book launch. His medal rests on his protruding beer gut beneath the words *I may be wrong, but I doubt it* emblazoned on his T-shirt.

Brian and Gary shake hands and we introduce our family.

"I saw you coming across the finish line. I didn't realise you're a runner," Fran says.

"I'm a late starter. I only began running this year for this event."

"Did you run the whole way?" Brian asks, studying me closely.

"Yep, that was my goal and we did it. I had some good cheer leaders to help me along the way." I smile at Ali and Michael before turning back to Brian. "How did you go?"

"Fran runs like a rabbit so I lost sight of her at the start line. I admit I walked most of it."

This admission makes me want to gloat and I check myself. I haven't been able to forget what he said about never being able to beat Parkinson's, but I don't want to be that person.

"How are you keeping?" Fran asks.

"I feel great. I've set myself a tough fitness programme and maintain a reasonable diet and am just generally well. I certainly can't complain."

"You are looking better than when I last saw you," Fran says. "Let's sit in the shade for a bit."

We wander across to the grass verge under a tree and sit down. We chat while watching the walkers come through the finish line, stopping every now and then to cheer them on. Today everyone is a champion. And today I feel like I have defeated Parkinson's disease.

Before parting company Brian moves closer to me and says quietly, "I think I owe you an apology."

"What for?"

"I said something inappropriate at the book launch. Do you remember?" His look is intense. "I said there's no point fighting Parkinson's, that it's got you."

"I remember." My voice sounds slightly incredulous.

"Well, I was wrong and you are living proof. You are obviously fighting it and you are looking much better. It's worth the fight."

I look at this man with the rosy cheeks and see him in a new light. It's a courageous thing for some people to admit they were wrong. "Thanks. That means a lot to me."

After parting company with Fran and Brian we search the official race results and find I ran the course in 53.4 minutes at an average pace of 6.23 minutes per km. That puts me in the top seven per cent for my gender and age group, able-bodied and all. I relish my achievement, even more so for having Parkinson's. I haven't felt this good for a long time and I'm filled with renewed hope—hope that I can slow the progression of the disease, hope that I can continue to do the things I love, hope that I have years before I really start to deteriorate, hope that a cure will be discovered in time.

The rest of the afternoon is spent chilling among the crowds. It's a party of thousands. Strangers who wouldn't normally mix unite under a common achievement and we soak it all up. We eventually find our way back to the car and head for home exhausted but elated. *So, take that Parkinson's!*

14

Rose, Marlborough Sounds, March 2020

I disembark from the boat and step onto Outward Bound's jetty at Anakiwa in the beautiful Queen Charlotte Sound. My excitement is mixed with apprehension, but I'm determined to give it my best shot. Along with the other eleven members of my watch we form a human chain to unload the luggage from the hold and on to the wharf. Chatter comes easily and although one hour ago we were strangers, a sense of team builds as we work together.

Our group consists of eleven men and women affected by young or early-onset Parkinson's disease and one person is there to support her husband who is on the course. We form the annual Parkinson's Watch that is sponsored by a trust established by a generous patron in partnership with Parkinson's New Zealand. Outward Bound is an outdoor education boot camp where participants are challenged beyond their comfort zones.

I'd known of Outward Bound since my teenage years when each year my father would sponsor an apprentice to take part in a course. Dad often talked about the positive impact the experience had on those young men. So impressed by these changes he and a couple of others established a trust fund for money raised by our district youth group, through organised dances, to send local kids to Outward Bound. I would have gone then if I was physically adventurous, but I declined the opportunity. Having Parkinson's has changed me in so many unexpected ways, and here I am.

With the bags now on the jetty I stop to take in my surroundings. The afternoon sun sparkles over the still, deep-aqua bay broken only by a dozen boats that sit idle on their moorings. Bush-covered hills rise steeply from the water's edge. It is peaceful except for the song of the tui and korimako. Dotted around the shore are a few remote settlements away from the busyness of urban life. A road follows the beach front of the sound and ends near the entrance to Outward Bound. Half a dozen campervans neatly line the road giving them easy access to the Queen Charlotte walking track.

"Hey everyone, can you please gather around in a small circle," Shelly calls. She'd introduced herself on the boat as one of our instructors.

We shuffle into a circle.

"You are the Huria Watch, named after Huria Matenga." She looks around the group. "Does anyone know why Huria was a local heroine?"

Blank faces and heads shaking side to side form the response.

Shelly continues, "Huria Matenga lived at Whakapuaka in the nineteenth century. In 1863 the ship Delaware ran aground on some rocks during a storm. Huria, with her husband and three other men, went to their rescue. She allegedly swam into the surf to pick up a line thrown by the captain. The storm was so fierce that the crew ended up in the water and she kept swimming out, rescuing many.

Only one crewman was lost in what could've been a total disaster." Shelly slowly looks around our group. "So it's a real honour to be called the Huria Watch."

Bravery is an important quality for Parkinson's patients. The cap fits.

Toni, another instructor, joins Shelly.

"Can you please get your luggage and line up in order of height," Toni says.

We take a few moments as we size one another up. I find I'm the tallest and move to the back of the line.

"When I call zero I want you to call out your number starting with one being the shortest and ending with the tallest. We'll be doing this to make sure we don't leave anybody behind." Toni beams her engaging smile at us. "Zero!"

"One!" "Two!" "Three!" "Four!" "Five!" "Six!" "Seven!" "Eight!" "Nine!" "Ten!" "Eleven!"

I lift my arms to the sky as I call, "Twelve!"

"Let's go!"

Toni and Shelly start walking towards the shore and we follow, hauling our luggage down the long jetty and across the road to the entrance of the Outward Bound school. We assemble in a space in front of the main building where another group are waiting for us so the formal welcome can start.

Let the adventure begin.

*

I wake up early and listen to the symphony of snores. We all share our bunk room, men and women alike, and I'm thankful for the ear plugs I'd thrown in with my gear.

Our shared alarm goes off too soon and we rouse ourselves to get into our running gear in preparation for our early morning PT. Looking bleary-eyed we assemble on the concourse and follow the PT instructor. Then it's out to the road for a 3.5 km run followed by a dip in the icy cold water of the sound.

After breakfast we're given instructions to prepare for a day out in the bush by collecting gear and making lunches. We pair up and share the packs. My inability to multi-task, remember lists and my dithering about frustrate me. Where has that competent multi-tasker gone?

Shelly gives me the task of leader and we follow the Queen Charlotte walking track along the bays to our lunch spot. Jen and I share a pack and by the time we stop for lunch my back is aching under its weight. After lunch our mission is to trek off-track through the bush and up to the highest point on the ridge to the north of the school in Anakiwa.

I try to pick the easiest route up the hill at a pace everyone can maintain. It's a challenging test for the fittest of us and even more so for those whose Parkinson's is more advanced. Those carrying packs up the hill have an even greater challenge. Jen takes her turn carrying our pack. She is small under its weight and Raymond insists on carrying it for her. Despite the steep and challenging terrain there's lots of chatter and laughter and a few tears. The team remain positive and constantly cajole one another. Once we reach the summit we stop to rest and share some snacks.

We follow a ridge track along the contour of the hills. Glimpses of deep-blue water appear through gaps in the bush. The scenes are breath taking. A steeply descending track leads us back down to the school. Jim, whose Parkinson's is more advanced, slips several times and I can see he's exhausted. He stubbornly refuses to hand over his pack and each time he falls he gets back up and, against all odds, carries on. I go extra slowly down the gnarly bits and point out any challenging roots or steep steps that make our way particularly difficult. Although completely spent Jim soldiers on. Today everyone is a hero, putting enormous effort in, but Jim is my superhero.

As we near the school a wild-looking ram comes hurtling towards Jim. Shelly sees a potential calamity unfold and runs to intercept. The ram reaches Jim and instead of bunting him it stands placidly and nuzzles him as if acknowledging his super-human effort.

"That's never happened before," Shelly says. "I thought it was going to attack. These sheep are fairly wild."

Jim's Parkie face is radiant, perfectly expressing a mountain conquered.

*

It's day three of our week at Outward Bound and we are led out into the bush to be dropped off one by one. We each have a pack with gear and food for twenty-four hours, a tent fly, ground sheet and a bucket for toileting to keep the bush pristine.

Toni leaves me in bush of wharangi, kanuka, pseudopanax and fern. I am alone with my pack. Not overly comfortable being on my own in the dark makes this my first real dragon to slay since arriving—a whole night going solo in the bush.

The sun has long since dropped below the hills and it's a race against darkness. I unload the tent fly and ground mat from under the top flap of my pack. I work quickly as I try to contain the apprehension that is rising inside me like a king tide that fills nooks and crannies and smothers everything in its path. I breathe in deeply to calm myself. Other members of my watch are camping solo along the track and several are within yelling distance. If I really need them they'd come running. *I can do this.*

After appraising the hard ground between the trees I select an area where the ground has the least slope to set up my camp. I choose a small tree and tie the cord from one end of the fly that will form the ridge around its trunk, thankful for the years of sailing that taught me how to tie knots. The choice of trees to tie the other end to is limited and the walking pole proves useful in deflecting the angle. It works and the ridge line of the fly runs along the flattest part of the slope with only a gentle roll downwards. Satisfied, I look around for something to tie down the corners of the fly. The light is fading rapidly, hastening a rummage through my pack for the headlight. Its beam attracts the insects as I move quickly about the campsite securing the corners and edges of the tent fly to ferns and scrub. With the fly in place and the long edges a mere thirty centimetres above the earth I finish by smoothing the ground sheet on the flat-but-sloping ground. It's not perfect. However, it will have to do.

My sleeping bag is in the bottom of the pack and I quickly pull everything out, eager to get sorted. My hands are clumsy when trying to operate the zip on the bag. Stress aggravates Parkinson's and my motor skills worsen. I fumble and try to steady my hands. *Take a deep breath.* At last the zip engages and the bag forms. I slip into my sleeping clothes and stuff everything back into the pack just in case a cheeky weka comes looking for something to steal during the night. At last I snuggle down into the sleeping bag and turn off the torch.

At first everything is pitch black in my campsite. When I look out through the gap under the fly the stars appear brighter and more numerous than usual. A satellite moves slowly across the night sky. My eyes adjust and my night vision develops. It's surprising how much is visible in the darkness around me. And yet I feel so vulnerable in the dark. It's the unseen that generates my fear. I pull the sleeping bag around me. Tightly. Trussed like a Christmas turkey with the headtorch wrapped around my wrist for reassurance and instant access, I silently pray for protection. *I can do this solo night in the bush. I will slay this dragon.*

Insects buzz in the darkness. In the distance and high in a tree a ruru calls *morepork*. My breathing slows and I feel secure in my sleeping bag. As my body warms the trapped air in the bag I wrestle my way out of my warm merino top and leggings. My skin becomes moist with the exertion and yet I'm too scared to open the sleeping bag's zip.

Stillness.

Water washes on rocks far below as a squall moves across the bay and rustles the bush as it makes its way up the hillside towards me. As it passes overhead my fly gently flaps and leaves drop from the trees above, sounding like rain.

Silence follows. My thoughts become vague and random.

Something wakes me. I press a button on my watch to light the screen and find I've been asleep for around an hour. A deep bellow sounds from somewhere up on the ridge. I tense and draw further into my sleeping bag. It roars again. Perhaps a bull or a cow bellowing in pain. But I know the hills that rise above Queen Charlotte are covered in bush and there are no farms. Another roar, further this time. It's the sound of a stag roaring for its mate. It isn't close and nor is it interested in me. I'm safe. I let out the breath I'm holding and snuggle down.

Movement in the nearby bush startles me and I immediately feel the adrenaline course through my body. Branches rustle and snap as something moves towards me. So close now I can hear it breathing. It sounds almost human. Panting accompanies a steady stream of water splashing on the ground as it urinates nearby. My body is poised in evolutionary terror—fight, flight or freeze. I freeze and hold my breath. I emerge from my momentary time capsule and decide it must be a hind deer. The bush rustles and more twigs snap as it moves away towards the call of the stag. I'm safe. She has no interest in me.

Another sound, this time from the immediate vicinity of my camp. A weka. I feel for my pack and draw it closer. I wait. I can just make out movement in the gloom. It moves away.

More roaring from somewhere on the ridge top. A second stag roars in response from a distant hilltop. And then the unmistakable rasping of an opossum, close. I pinpoint the new noise to the branches above my tent fly. I tell myself it's more afraid of me than I am of it. I lie still, listening.

They said it will be a time for self-reflection. That doesn't seem likely as I'm too scared to think beyond surviving this night.

Moisture coats my skin as the heat inside the sleeping bag becomes unbearable. I unzip it and fan cool air into the bag. Now my bare arms are exposed, but my head remains inside the hood as the thought of something crawling through my hair is too much. I shudder, pull my arms back inside and zip it up again leaving only the area around my eyes exposed.

A new sound fills the silence. It's close and noisier than all the other sounds of the night bush. It conveys urgent movement and the hair along the nape of my neck stands as my body sweats out its fear. It moves towards me grunting and snorting. My stomach twists and tightens as I imagine a wild boar with sharp tusks rooting around in the undergrowth. The hair along my spine prickles with unease like a spider crawling along one vertebra at a time. I try to decide if I should flash it with my headlight, whether the light will frighten it off or attract it to me. Instinct tells me that of all the creatures in the night this one will not be frightened by my presence. This one could walk straight through my campsite. This one could attack me. I am so vulnerable lying here defenceless in my sleeping bag. I stay quiet in the dark hoping it will go away. I wait.

A buried memory surfaces. Lying on the ground being strangled, my life at the mercy of a stranger. I can almost taste the bile that comes with terror. I pray. And I pray. I contemplate my fear—the real dragon I need to slay.

There is no place in me for the spirit of fear. I am a child of the light. My inheritance is the spirit of love through grace and with that comes the gifts of love, joy and peace. This is where my strength comes from. Fear is no more than perception. It's like darkness itself. Shine the light on it and it is nothing. Like a whim or a folly, fear has no substance unless I allow it a foothold and only then will it steal my joy and steal my peace. I hold the power to control it with my response. I will not let it win. I will not be afraid.

Peace slowly settles over me replacing my fear. The sound of the wild pig recedes into the distance. I open the zip on my sleeping bag again allowing the cool air to gently kiss my skin. It's five a.m. The cry of *morepork* pierces the darkness. I'm safe among the cacophony of the bush. I open the sleeping bag further, no longer needing to be cocooned. I wait in anticipation of the dawn chorus.

As the splendour of the first red rays of dawn light up the hilltops, the birds sing their chorus heralding my achievement. I've overcome my fear and survived my first night out in the bush. Shuffling out of my sleeping bag I stand to watch the dawn, stretching my stiff body and letting my euphoria fill the spaces where fear resided only a few hours ago.

With dawn comes the deafening chorus of a million cicadas.

I dump my pack contents in a heap on the ground sheet and select clothes for the day before changing and eating some of my breakfast rations. I'm careful not to leave any bits lying about so my new flatmate, whom I name *Willie Weka*, can't steal them. I work slowly—I have all day. The tent fly is now rearranged to provide shade with one side open so I can sit and drink in the view over the bush and the water below. It's a camp with a view and it won't be hard to spend the day here away from life's busyness, just being in the moment, being mindful.

I open the little black journal given to record our thoughts and start my homework. We were instructed to write two letters—one to our sponsors and one to ourselves. I play with the pencil as I consider what to write.

The letter to myself is simple—*Just do it!* I silently thank Nike for their slogan and consider how much I've changed thanks to Parkinson's. If it wasn't for this affliction I would not be here at Anakiwa. I would never have slain my dragon last night. I would not have learned that the only limitation I have is what I place on myself. Now thankful I decide to make a list of the positives that early-onset Parkinson's has gifted me.

I've a whole new circle of friends who are fellow Parkie sufferers. We have become close because of our shared experiences. Without Parkinson's I wouldn't have met them. And to me they are inspirational heroes. Parkinson's is not for the faint-hearted and everyone living with it is a hero. I'm grateful to have them in my life. I write:

1. New Parkie friends who inspire me

My diagnosis has led me to a fitness crusade that's improved my general wellness and has made me fitter and stronger than I've ever been. I feel younger, more confident, more adventurous and more willing to take on new physical challenges, like being at Outward Bound.

2. Better fitness, strength, confidence and more adventurous

Having Parkinson's has led me to take early retirement, reducing the stress in my life. It's led us to rethink our retirement plans and now Gary is also planning to retire early so we can enjoy retired life while we both have good health. We're less focused on working hard and squirrelling away for some future time that may never eventuate and more focused on living now. It's an unexpected gift of freedom from the trappings of our culture.

3. Less stress

4. Early retirement while we can enjoy it in good health

I put my pencil down and stop to listen to the clear song of a korimako, its exquisite melody hanging in the air like perfectly-tuned tubular bells. My eyes search the trees and I find the little green bird on a branch overhanging my camp site. A second korimako answers and I savour the moment—joy, where only hours earlier lay fear. I pick up my pencil and return my attention to my notebook.

I'm far more appreciative of the life I have. My diagnosis has shown me how quickly things can change and I'm more thankful for the small things in my day. Things that in the past I barely noticed, things I can see, smell, hear, taste or touch. Life can be good even with Parkinson's if I let it. It's my choice how I respond to it.

5. Living in the moment and taking time to appreciate the small things

The last few days with my watch team has shown how we are each having to use extra initiative, often having to find new and novel ways to overcome the minefield of difficulties created by the disease.

6. Gifted with extra initiative

I chew my pencil as I consider another positive. Parkinson's has given me a new crusade on two levels. The first is to know and fight my adversary. The second is my desire to help others with Parkinson's by sharing the hope that I have and to demonstrate we can live positively with Parkinson's disease.

7. New purpose, to study and fight PD
8. Desire to help other Parkies

I stop writing and sit very still, intent on absorbing the beauty around me, intent on just being.

A piwakawaka flits around a silver fern chasing insects for breakfast. It dips and dives, darts and turns. If I could fly I would want to fly like the little piwakawaka. Its tail feathers fan wide like a perfect scallop shell, the dark centre feathers flanked on both sides with pale ones. It lands on the edge of a frond, its head to one side, watching me with dark eyes, its expression impish under the little white marks that look like eyebrows. Around its neck is a collar of white and another of black, perfectly adorning its tan underbelly. No sooner has it rested than it flits away again to explore the edges of my campsite.

Our watch is a close-knit team bound by a thread that is our common foe, Parkinson's disease. We are in the trench facing our common enemy, but we are not alone in the battle. Having compassion for each other makes us a tight team. Compassion is to suffer with another and I've been inspired by the wealth of compassion shown on this watch and by my Parkinson's friends.

I pick up my notebook and pencil and add another positive to my list.

9. I'm learning to be more compassionate.

I finish my list of positives and write *Thanks Parkinson's!*

A weka scurries out of the low scrub on sturdy legs, its fat body coated in rich brown feathers flecked with black and grey. For a moment it holds my gaze with its red eyes before hurrying back into the bush.

The continuous chirping of cicadas is broken with a whooshing sound as a kereru swoops overhead, its clumsy wingbeat unmistakable. Although its flight is adequate for it to thrive in the bush it lacks the graceful flight of other birds. As it settles on a branch rays of sunlight highlight the sheen of its shiny green-purple feathers that are in stark contrast to its white underbelly. Perhaps impaired motor skills make us Parkies the kereru of the human world. That wouldn't be so bad. I write:

There is no need to fear my future living with Parkinson's. I just need to be the best that I can physically be today and the future can take care of itself. I know that I can live positively—even with this thorn in my side. It will not define me and it will not rob me of my joy and my peace.

*

"I want you all to think of a mantra that you can tell yourself when facing a fight, flight or freeze situation," Toni says. "And I want you to remember it when we are doing today's activity."

Our watch is gathered in a room in the main building and Toni has just talked about how our brains work when facing danger or stress. It's our last full day at Outward Bound.

I look at my shoes. Thanks Nike. *Just do it!*

"Let's go!"

Our watch is quiet as we follow Toni towards the edge of the camp for our next challenge. I catch the odd furtive glance and realise I'm not the only nervous one. Although I haven't seen a high ropes course around the complex there must be one or else we could be going rock climbing. Either way I will have to face my fear of heights. My gut tightens. And yet I am unexpectedly eager to face another of my dragons and I want to slay this one. *Just do it!*

We find our other instructors in a grove of kahikatea armed with helmets, harnesses and other safety equipment. Above us is a high ropes course with wires approximately twelve metres above the ground. A crashing sound comes from the canopy high above as a pair of kereru fly between trees. These guardians of the bush coo as if they are watching over us Parkies, almost as if they know we will soon be up in their domain. Our sentinels.

We are helped into our gear and Shelly explains the course to us.

"Who wants to be first?" asks Ariel, an Israeli instructor.

I want to overcome this dragon and so without a moment's hesitation I call out, "I will."

"Good for you." Ariel checks my safety gear.

"I'm terrified of heights although I really want to smash this. I want to be able to go home and surprise my family by climbing to the top of the mast on our boat. I've never had the courage to do that."

"Okay, let's do this."

I stand at the bottom of the wire ladder and watch him climb. Following, I get halfway up and pause. It's a long way down and the ladder sways slightly with each step. Doubts creep in. *Just do it!* I take another step. And then another. Soon I am at the top transferring my carabiner to the wire for the first section of the course.

Mary and Me

"Give her some extra challenges," Shelly calls from below.

Her meaning isn't clear and I assume she's bluffing. My tremor becomes more intense. My legs feel weak.

Ariel moves across the first wire and makes it look easy. I take a step, my foot as close to perpendicular to the wire as I can place it. Then another and another. I hear the clapping and encouragement from my friends below.

"Fall into your safety harness," Ariel says.

The safety harness takes my weight while I hang there feeling as safe as I can allow myself to be. Then somehow I manage to haul myself back up and move to the tree where Ariel waits. He shows me how to transfer my safety harness to the next section before he duck-walks with ease to the next tree. I try to follow his lead, but my feet stick to the wire.

"I'm stuck," I confess.

"You can do it. Keep coming," he says.

I'm clumsy now and my left leg is vibrating wildly with tremor. "I'm trying." *Just do it.*

Ariel gently encourages me on. I focus on my feet, only just aware of the encouraging words coming from below. I reach the tree and transfer my carabiners.

The next section requires walking a suspended log. Ariel walks it without holding on and makes it look easy. My balance is challenged and I'm not sure I could walk a log even if it were lying on the ground let alone when suspended twelve metres above. I prepare to take a step, but nothing happens. I clutch my safety harness.

"Let go of your harness," he coaxes.

I let it go but stay frozen. *Just do it.* Again I try to take a step, but my legs won't move.

More encouragement.

The left side of my body tremors uncontrollably and my gut clenches tight. Perhaps this was all a bad idea. *Just do it.* I'm no quitter. This is my dragon to slay. I clutch my safety harness rope and take one step, then another.

"Let go!"

I let the harness rope go and take the last few steps until I can reach for the tree. I make it and with that my confidence grows. *I can do this.*

The next section has me leap between platforms.

"Now leap backwards," Ariel says.

I can't bring myself to do so. With a deep breath I leap across sideways. Twice.

I get part way across the swinging ropes section.

"Stop there. See the tree to your left?" Ariel is pointing to a kahikatea that stands straight and tall.

"Yes." I size up the trunk that stands just out of my reach.

"Your extra challenge is to leap out and hug the tree with your hands and feet."

I know he wouldn't issue a challenge unless he knows it's safe, but there's a great gulf between me and the tree.

"Do it Rose," Shelly calls from below.

Just do it! I don't want to give in to fear. *I can do this.* I jump out to the tree and wrap my arms and legs around it, tightly. Applause comes from below and I can feel the tension go out of my body as I become an avid tree hugger.

"Well done. Now just swing back."

With a firm grip on the swinging rope I push off the tree, my back leg finding the wire. Mustering all my strength I haul myself upright with the rope. Made it. Now more than halfway around the course I know I can do this. And I'm nailing it.

"Now turn to your right," Ariel says. "See the skinny tree a metre and a half away from you? I want you to hug that one."

"You must be joking!" I shake my head in disbelief.

"No I'm not. Lean out like you are going to fall and catch it."

"No way!"

"You can do it. Just trust yourself."

I size up the tree. This is one challenge too many, but I desperately want to succeed. My tremor amplifies. The challenge is my nemesis, my disease. *Just do it!*

Leaning out I push off and, just as I begin to fall, grab at the tree and wrap myself around it. Joy and tears of relief. It's not that I'm unsafe—I know my harness will keep me safe even if I fall—it's overcoming my fear and achieving the challenge even when every fibre in me wants to take the easy road. I hear the encouragement from below and I look down, beaming. Then I turn my attention back to the task ahead. Somehow I manage to get back on the wire and traverse the remainder of the swinging ropes section.

"Good work," Ariel says. "I'm not going to help you with the climbing board. I want you to find your own way across it."

With that he makes his way across it like a monkey and stands against the tree at the other side.

"Your turn."

I gingerly put my foot onto the first foothold and grab a hand grip. It's not as easy as Ariel made it look and my left leg is too clumsy to get it through the gap to the next foothold. I move back to the tree and start again. *I can do this!* I strain with all my strength and manage to move first one foot, then one hand, the other foot, the other hand. I keep going.

About one third of the way across I experience pain and call out to Ariel, "My arms have cramped."

"Rest for a minute. You can lean into your harness," he instructs.

I do as he says and shake out my arms, bitterly disappointed to have failed the last challenge. *Just do it!*

I reach for the handholds and pull myself back onto the board, movement by movement, centimetre by centimetre, grunting at each exertion. *I will do this!* I reach for the last foothold, just one more handhold and … I pull myself onto the platform next to Ariel.

Thank you, Lord. The prayer is silent on my breath.

"You're a fighter." He grins.

"That's one dragon that won't be breathing fear anymore."

Euphoria inflates my body and I become as light as a feather. Gone is my tremor. I have just slain another dragon, proving once more that fear has no place in my life. There are no limitations to what I can achieve except those that I place on myself. With hard work I can overcome. *Just do it!*

"Now you get to enjoy the flying fox." He sets me up and I whizz down the wire to my Huria Watch friends waiting at the bottom.

I conquered the high ropes course. *Take that Parkinson's!*

*

It's the last day and we stand out by the jetty, our luggage stacked beside the road, waiting for the boat that will ferry us back to the Picton terminal and our daily lives.

I absorb the peaceful setting, the aqua-blue water and the bush-covered hills. It's hard to believe we've been here only a week, yet I am changed forever. I have discovered things in me that will help me face whatever lies ahead.

When I signed up for Outward Bound I wanted to be challenged out of my comfort zone, to become more resilient and confident and better prepared to fight for my well-being. I have not been disappointed. I was also looking forward to making new friends and to being part of a team again, and I've achieved this in spades. We've become more than a team, more like a family. We've cajoled and teased, shared laughter and tears. I'm confident these will be lasting friendships.

My most shocking revelation has been seeing how much my cognitive skills have deteriorated. When preparing for the activities, such as packing for the solo in the bush, our instructors gave us clear instructions and put us under time pressure. My attention span, my ability to follow instructions, my recall of details and ability to multi-task have been particularly challenged, especially when distracted. I've found I can easily lose track of what I'm doing. I've seen this same trait to varying degrees in my watch mates and I know it's related to Parkinson's, either a symptom or a side-effect of the drugs. A film of a group of Parkies trying to carry out multiple instructions under time pressure would provide lots of good material for a black comedy.

I arrived at Outward Bound reasonably fit and strong, the result of three years of determination, self-discipline and hard work. My watchmates have helped me to see how good my symptoms really are. More importantly I was unprepared for how much I would be inspired by them, especially those who are more physically challenged. They've applied themselves to the physical trials with true grit and determination. They've maintained a positive attitude in the face of what, at times, appeared to be real adversity. It's in this spirit that I need to fight the disease every day for as long as I live or until the cure is available.

Our instructors join us and Huria Watch stand in front to perform one final act. With grins like Cheshire cats we sing:

"Zero One Two Three Four Five Six Seven Eight Nine Ten Eleven Twelve

> *We are Huria Watch from afar*
> *We are all a new whanau*
> *Rise and shine at crack of dawn*
> *You don't know what you're in for*
> *PT run and icy swim*
> *Followed by a cold shower*
> *Bush trek, sailing, solo challenge,*
> *Climbing, falling, it's a breeze*
> *TAKE THAT PARKINSON'S*

Zero One Two Three Four Five Six Seven Eight Nine Ten Eleven Twelve
Huria Watch!"

15

James, London, 1814

Four years elapse before I encounter Mary Black again. It is a dismal grey London day and a damp mist hangs heavily over the city. On such a day as this I would prefer to be in front of the hearth enjoying the pleasures of a pipe stuffed with rich tobacco and a good book. Alas it is a workday and I have reason to visit St Luke's Hospital for Lunatics where one of my patients is in temporary residence.

I step out onto the cobbled street, my coat pulled close around my neck against the chill and my top hat snug on my head. A cab drawn by a scrawny white horse comes towards me and I lift my stick to hail it.

"Whoa!" The driver pulls on the reins and the wretched animal draws to a stop.

"St Luke's Hospital on Old Street," I command the driver and climb aboard to settle into my seat, my bag clasped on my lap.

The regular clip clopping of the hoofs and the rocking of the wheels over the cobbles lull me into a reverie, broken only too soon as we draw up outside the high and foreboding brick wall that separates the asylum from the street. I disembark, tossing the driver a coin before he cracks his whip and disappears into the mist.

I pass through the St Luke's gate and pause, impressed by the expansive brick building. It is a magnificent structure with two symmetrical wings, the one to the left housing the male patients and to the right the female patients. There are rows of arched windows on each floor along the facade and a square tower at either end. This charitable institution was built by wealthy benefactors whose primary mandate is to accept the poor and mad aged between twelve and seventy.

A severe-looking woman sits at the reception desk. Her hair is parted and drawn under a lace cap, her black gown finished with thick black embroidery and a white lace collar.

"Good afternoon. I'm Doctor James Parkinson and am here to meet with my patient, Mrs Emily Blackfriar."

"Good afternoon, Doctor. We have Mrs Blackfriar waiting in the visitors' parlour. I will take you down there."

She rises, turns on her heel and proceeds down the cavernous hallway, her shoes noisy on the polished floor. We stop at a closed door while she draws a key out from the folds of her skirt and unlocks it. Once it is secured again I follow her along a corridor in the direction of the women's wards. We enter a small room with a wooden bench seat along one wall and two wooden chairs in front of a fireplace in the middle of the opposite wall. A miserable fire provides little cheer and is losing its battle to warm the room. The only light comes from the glow of the fire and a single small window.

My patient stands looking out the window and into the garden beyond. Her silhouette is tall and excessively thin; I swear she has become even thinner while staying at this institution. Since the tragic death of her child, she has been plagued with excessive lamentation to the point of causing harm to herself and threatening to harm her other children. The sooner she is stabilised the sooner she can return home.

She turns to face me with a look that conveys deep emotional pain. I finger the inside of my tight collar and wish there were more I could do to help her. The good Lord knows how much her family need her.

The consultation does not take long and I soon find I am taking my leave. Opening the door into the corridor I begin to retrace my steps. A door to one of the single cells is open and I peer in. It has a small window set high in the wall and loose straw is on a wooden bedstead. There is no hearth, no heating. A small woman shakes violently in a rocking chair with wheels and I stop to study her more closely. Her shoulders are hunched forward, her head droops at an impossible angle and saliva drools from her lips. The tremors rack her body cruelly and she seems unaware of my presence.

"Good afternoon, Madam." I tip my hat and bow in her direction.

She lifts her head slightly, enough to peer up at me with unblinking blue eyes, her face a mask like those I have observed as part of the shaking palsy condition. Something in this small oval face is familiar. It is the Hoxton woman whom I had chanced upon and interviewed in Hoxton Square some four years earlier. Her palsy has progressed leaving her in a pitiful state. I note something else—a haunted and frightened look.

"I remember you from Hoxton. I once interviewed you and enquired about your condition," I say.

She appears to rouse herself from her private hell and I detect a faint flicker of recognition in her dull eyes although she is struck dumb.

I try again. "Mrs Black isn't it?"

There it is again—that flicker of recognition. Then, almost imperceptibly, she answers, "Yes, sir." Her eyes water and a single tear escapes and runs down her sallow cheek.

Footsteps in the corridor hurry towards me.

A nurse enters. "Excuse me Doctor, I need to take Mrs Black for her plunge bath."

The patient flinches and becomes agitated and I am filled with sympathy. A cold plunge bath is believed to shake lunatics out of their insanity, but this patient is not insane. I am certain this condition is a palsy and cannot be taken out of her. I am likewise of the opinion that the other common treatments to remove the insanity, such as medications to induce vomiting and suppositories, will also not remove this palsy.

"Please nurse," I implore. "This treatment will not help this condition. Let me speak to her physician."

"Sir, this is her treatment time and I must take her to the bath now."

I look at the nurse whose face is set in harsh lines and I know I must leave her to her duty.

Turning to the patient I tip my hat. "Mrs Black, I bid you farewell."

I walk the length of the corridor and am let out through the locked door. I hurry outside, eager to escape the misery within the brick walls. A carriage waits near the entrance, however I am too troubled to hail it. Pulling my coat in more tightly against the cold I begin to walk in the direction of my rooms.

The poor and pitiful soul, Mrs Black, causes me much distress. My observations of this horrible malady convince me that she is not insane. Thankfully she is not suffering the added shame of being restrained as her physical condition makes it impossible for her to walk unaided. The patients in the asylum generally remain in care until cured, but with no cure for her condition this will be her life until she takes her last breath.

The bleak cold weather reflects my miserable mood. Puddles have formed on the cobbles. A carriage passes at a pace and the wheels flick water over my coat. I clutch my bag more tightly and walk faster, eager to get home to the comfort of my sanctuary.

For the next few days I go about my business with a weight on my heart. Not even my collection of fossils and shells can bring me pleasure. As a physician I am dedicated to the science of healing and to stand by and watch human suffering is unbearable. For some inexplicable reason this poor soul known as Mrs Mary Black has penetrated the very depths of my own soul and I am tormented.

I am due a visit to my dear sister, Elizabeth, who lives to the north of Hoxton in the countryside. Long since widowed, Elizabeth lives alone in her husband's house on the outskirts of Tottenham. I make the arrangements and know a weekend with my sister will do much to restore my good humour.

It is not long to wait until I am in the coach as it bumps its way north. It is a beautiful spring day. The air is still and the sun shines brightly. The light greens of new

Mary and Me

growth on the trees and in the meadows are vivid in the sunlight. The hedgerows are alive with small birds and the occasional rabbit. Inside the coach I share in pleasant conversation with two other gentlemen passengers and the time passes quickly.

We trot into Tottenham and I am greatly relieved to see Elizabeth, an elegant woman of a sunny and gentle disposition, standing at the coach stop. She wears the black of mourning, a velvet coat decorated with embroidery and fastened at the bust over a long black skirt. At the neck is a ruffled lace collar that frames her beautiful face. Her dark, curly hair peeks out from under her cream bonnet that is edged with matching lace.

I step down from our carriage and eagerly embrace her. "My dear sister, just look at you. My, you have the cheeks of a farmer's wife."

"And you, brother, the pallor of the city."

I have always loved the banter of siblings and already my spirit is somewhat restored. I collect my bag and bid my farewells to my travelling companions. Elizabeth and I walk over to a small carriage that is waiting for us. After a short fifteen-minute ride we are pulling up outside her home, a pretty cottage set in a garden of blossoms and colour dotted amongst the shrubbery.

"Sister, this is tonic indeed!"

Elizabeth leads me inside and waits while I refresh from my journey. I join her for tea and sandwiches in the parlour. We have much to catch up on and I listen with interest as she describes her charity work with the local parish.

"Another sandwich, brother?"

"Please."

She passes the plate and as I take another sandwich she asks, "And what about you? How is your work?"

"My clinic is busy as I do not discriminate between the classes. There is much fever and smallpox among my patients and for many it is a matter of making their last days comfortable and trying to stem the spread. Colic, pleurisy, accidents, convulsions and melancholy are common ailments; these I can help. As for childbirth, it is a joy to preside over the healthy birth of an infant and see the mother recover and rear the child." I pause and look out the small windowpane into the garden seeing nothing other than the image of Mary Black. I sip my tea.

"What is it brother? I detect something bothers you."

My gaze returns to my sister. "Yes, you are right. I have been struck by a melancholy that I cannot seem to dislodge. I have noticed a new species of disease among my patients and on the streets. I believe it to be a type of palsy, a shaking palsy, a disabling condition that progresses with time. There is no cure for these poor wretches and many are stigmatised with accusations of too much liquor or even demonic causes. It is something I have observed although it is not yet understood. I am convinced it is a nervous disorder."

"Then James, that is good is it not? You could change this."

"I do not have any idea of how to cure it, but I feel compelled to write an essay on my findings. I have been carefully documenting my observations on their trembling, their posture and their gait. At the very least these sufferers need to know it is an ailment and it should be identified as such."

"Then that should be immensely satisfying for you. It could change their lives." Elizabeth cocks her head to one side and beams.

"There's more." I look at my hands now clasped in my lap.

"Pray tell."

Slowly, taking care not to leave out any details, I relate the story of Mary Black. I tell of my first encounter when interviewing her in Hoxton Square and finally our encounter in St Luke's Hospital for Lunatics. Elizabeth sits patiently, watching me closely while absorbed in my story.

"Brother, that poor soul. What can you do to help her?"

"I honestly don't know. It sits heavy on my mind. She deserves better than her current treatment." I look my sister in the eye and add quietly, "I feel partly to blame."

"Oh James, that is untrue. Why should you possibly feel any guilt?"

"As a physician I feel we are letting her down. She is afflicted by a condition in her nervous system, an ailment that is entirely not of her making. And yet she is being punished because we are ignorant of its very existence." I shake my head from side to side.

We are silent for a while.

"James, I have an idea." Elizabeth claps her delicate hands and sits on the very edge of her chair, her green eyes shining.

"Well?" I'm intrigued by the sudden change in her.

"Why don't you bring her to me? I need to find greater purpose for my life. I have my charity work, but I also have time, lots of time. And I am blessed with this house. I can nurse her and tend to her. While we were growing up I observed how Mother assisted Father with his patients. I can do this. Do please let me help."

I am stunned. This sister of mine never ceases to amaze me and her compassion knows no bounds. I think of poor Mary Black, of the small cell that confines her, of the cold plunge bath treatments. Then I picture her lying in a bed chair on a day like today enjoying the garden with its flowers and bird song.

We talk further about the possibility of moving Mary Black to Tottenham. Elizabeth is adamant. The more we discuss it the more plausible it becomes and the shadow that has been hanging over me begins to lift.

My stay is brief and all too soon I am heading back to Hoxton. I find my spirit is transformed and I am eager to make more enquiries into the plight of Mary Black.

Over the next two weeks I determine that Mrs Mary Black has been abandoned by family and friends. She seldom speaks and her only human contact is with the nurses who deliver her treatment and spoon feed her. I make the necessary arrangements to have her transferred to my care and I arrange for a nurse to accompany her to Tottenham where she is taken to Elizabeth's house. A week later I receive a letter from Elizabeth to say that Mary Black is now settled into her care.

It is another month before I get an opportunity to visit Elizabeth. This time I make my way to her house alone. The countryside sparkles under the summer sun. I eagerly disembark as soon as my carriage pulls up in front of her cottage. There is a chair on the lawn under a large magnolia tree and I recognise the slight figure of Mary Black.

The front door opens and Elizabeth comes running down the path. Her black mourning garb is replaced by a green dress, its short sleeves trimmed with lace and fronted with a white apron. A white bonnet with a green ribbon tames her curls.

"James!" She plants a kiss on my cheek.

I hold her at arm's length and look at her for a moment. Her green eyes sparkle and her smile is relaxed.

"I see you're out of mourning," I say.

"Oh James, you must come and see Mary. She is doing so well." She takes my hand and leads me over to the chair. "Mary, I think you know my brother."

Mary looks up at me. Although her face is a mask her eyes appear to show recognition. She doesn't speak.

That evening Elizabeth entertains us with a piano recital and song. Her voice is like that of an angel. Mary does not take her eyes off her and appears to croon softly to the melody.

During the two days of my visit I observe Elizabeth tending to Mary Black with patience and kindness. Mary seems settled, even peaceful in her environment. Elizabeth is at great pains to bathe Mary and keep her clean and tidy. Mary loves her hair being brushed and responds with a sound that is best likened to a purr. Her skin, once pale and translucent, has a healthier glow from her time in the garden. Her blue eyes, previously dull, contain a light and at times I detect the suggestion of a smile on her face that convinces me she is happy here with Elizabeth. And on occasions I have even heard her utter a word of appreciation.

While I can never cure her, I know that through Elizabeth, Mary can live out her life with dignity and in the care that she deserves. I only wish for more Elizabeths to tend to the Marys of this world. I only wish there was more I could do to relieve Mary of her symptoms.

As God is my witness I will continue to fight for the Marys of this world.

16

Rose, Auckland, August 2020

"She's a beauty." I look at the gleaming white campervan with its stylised silver fern motif taking pride of place on its side.

"Sure is. What say you? Shall we do it?" Gary asks, a wide grin plastered across his face.

We have been looking at second-hand campervans with the idea that we will literally drive off into the sunset. Over the past few months we've hatched a cunning plan, one that will enable us to take an early retirement and live off the rent from our house. Gary came across a beautifully illustrated book that outlines the 100 best day walks in New Zealand, and that has become our goal. They span the country from the top of the north to Stewart Island in the south as well as from east to west. The walks are generally four to six hours in length and are of varying difficulty. They boast the best of New Zealand scenery and that means some of the best scenery in the world. Once we've exhausted the day walks there're also the great walks to explore, those that require overnighting in huts. We are so incredibly blessed to have such opportunities in our own backyard.

"Let's do it," I say. "Carpe diem!"

The camper is well used having been an ex-rental. It's in good condition and the layout is perfect, with the bed over the cab and windows around the back giving it an airy and spacious feel. There's plenty of storage and I can see us happily living in it as gypsies for a year or more.

The vendor talks us through the details of how things work while I try to contain my rising excitement. We started looking at campers only a couple of weeks ago with the intention of buying one early next year. And while this is only the fifth we've viewed, for some reason this is the one.

We sign the necessary papers and leave it there to have a few things done to it before taking ownership. The salesman looks pleased with himself at having secured the sale and Gary doesn't stop grinning.

Back in the car Gary says, "We'd better call the kids and let them know we've spent their inheritance money."

I make the phone call to Lauren and she answers on the third ring.

"Hello there. Dad and I thought we should tell you we just spent your inheritance on a campervan."

She chuckles. "You two are funny. I thought you said you were only looking and didn't want to buy until early next year?"

"We did and we didn't intend to buy one yet, but we fell in love with this one and think it's a good buy."

"That's awesome. So you really are going through with your early retirement plan."

"Yes, we want to have the time to do what we always dreamed we'd do while we are both healthy enough to do it."

"I'm really happy for you. What's it like?"

I outline the details of the campervan before adding, "You and Paul can borrow it anytime, that is, anytime we aren't using it. After all it's your inheritance money."

We laugh.

"We'd love to. When can we see it?"

"We pick it up next week and can drive by your place then."

"I love the way you guys are making the most of your lives. You seem to be living more in the moment than I remember from childhood. Back then you always seemed to be busy working. I think Parkinson's, for all its negatives, has given you a precious gift that's changed you in a way that has shown you how to get the most out of each day."

"I understand what you're saying and you're right. Having Parkinson's is the only reason we've bought a campervan now and the only reason we're contemplating early retirement. It means we won't have as much in savings later, but at least we'll get to enjoy our time now."

"Good on you guys. You've certainly got our support."

We talk some more and catch up on all that's been happening since our last chat before we end the call.

"She's right," Gary says. "There are some blessings in having an early diagnosis. I'm going to be counting down the days until we can take off. We may not know what lies ahead for you, but let's just enjoy each day. After all it may not be Parkinson's that stops us living our dream. It could be any number of things. We're not guaranteed a future and we're not guaranteed an easy ride, but we can choose to enjoy each moment."

"It's coming up four years since my diagnosis, at least six years since the tremor became persistent and nearly 25 years since I started experiencing the intermittent tremor, which I have to assume was an early sign. I know I'm lucky my version is a relatively mild form, but I never expected to feel this good. I really do feel better now than I did at the time I was diagnosed thanks to all the prayer, drugs, exercise and diet. I still feel like I've picked up my mat and am walking to a cure, if not a full cure then at least towards stopping the disease in its tracks. I have hope, lots of hope."

Gary reaches across and takes my hand. "I too have hope. I think the walking with the mat analogy is a good one. You are certainly doing your part and are not just sitting waiting for the disease to engulf you. It's been a journey to get to where we are now, but we've both grown in the process and we just need to take things one day at a time while helping you manage the symptoms as they come up."

"Hope is so important to staying positive and living well. To live without it would be like living life inside a cloud. There's really no choice."

"You're so right."

"I need to get my exercise in daily. I've been slack over the last couple of days and I'm sure my body shakes more and I feel generally lousy. It always seems to happen when I miss out on some intense exercise."

"It shows you need to stay disciplined. Let's get a walk in when we get home."

The phone chirps and I answer it.

"Hello there. Did you see the van?" Dad's voice comes across the airways.

"Hi Dad. We are indeed the proud owners of a campervan."

"Really?" His voice has genuine surprise. "You two are impetuous. Are you bringing it home with you now?"

"No, the vendor is going to do a few things to it for us before we pick it up. Should be ready next week."

"I have a surprise myself."

"What's that?" I look at Gary and wink. "Has one of those ladies at the retirement village asked you out?"

"Don't be silly!" His tone is sharp.

I smile, thinking how naïve he is. A single man as competent as him living in a retirement village would make a fine catch for one of the numerous single ladies on the hunt for a companion and partner.

"So what's up?" I ask.

"I've heard back from the ancestry outfit in the UK. It appears my great-great-grandmother was buried in a graveyard near Tottenham. Alone. What would you make of that?"

"That's odd. Are you sure it's her?"

"The dates marry up. And it says she is wife of John Black."

"The mystery deepens. Did the ancestry people have any ideas?"

"No they didn't offer any."

"It might be worth doing a Google search on how people with Parkinson's were treated in the Georgian era. Even today in remote areas of Africa where the education is not so good, people with tremor symptoms are often treated with superstition and it can even be associated with witchcraft. I wonder if the same was true for Georgian England?"

"Maybe, but how would she have ended up in Tottenham?"

"You may need to accept that it's a mystery you cannot solve." He doesn't reply and I add, "At least if it's a recorded death it doesn't imply anything untoward happened to her."

"I wouldn't think so."

"It's fascinating though. I can see why people get hooked on following their family trees."

He pumps me about the campervan and I give the details. Then in typical Dad fashion he abruptly ends the call making the excuse he needs to get on and make his dinner.

After a call to Michael we arrive home and decide to go out for a walk having not had the chance to exercise during the day. We walk at a fast pace along the hills near our home and take in the views over the ocean. It's a calm evening and the sun is low in the sky spreading golden colour over the water and warming the green tones of the foliage.

"I'm trying to practise swinging my arm in time to my feet, but as soon as I think about it the timing gets all muddled," I say. "And yet if I concentrate on the good arm and just relax the shaky one I can swing it and the timing is about right. It's so weird."

"There's so much more to understand about Parkinson's. I'm sure there's a lot we can do to find workarounds and manage some of the symptoms."

"I agree. The brain is such a complex organ and seems to be so poorly understood."

"Since your diagnosis I've seen you shocked, scared, anxious, weakened, vulnerable, angry, frustrated, insatiably curious, determined, disciplined, resilient, tough, compassionate, inspirational and victorious." Gary punctuates the words with a series of puffs as we navigate the steep part of the hill.

I laugh. "Now that's quite a list. Have you been studying a dictionary?"

"It's true and I've probably missed some of the obvious ones. My point is that it's been a huge rollercoaster both physically and emotionally. Now all your effort, discipline and sheer stubborn determination is bearing fruit. As well as that all the evidence from research and personal experience that shows you can change your prognosis is overwhelming. It's a message that needs to get out there."

"I think it is getting out slowly. But remember I'm lucky to have an early diagnosis at a stage when I can still put in the hard work."

We walk on in silence for a few minutes.

"I've just figured it out." I slow down and turn to him. "While I will continue to fight the disease with everything in my arsenal, my real nemesis is not so much the disease but the fear it generates. My greatest fear is of the unknown, fear of what the future holds and fear that I'll lose my independence and become a burden. Like when at Outward Bound I can deal to the fear. Fear is merely perception, but it will destroy hope if I let it. It's only real if I allow it to consume my mind. I can beat it."

"So that's the real dragon you need to slay." Gary places his arm across my shoulders. "If there's an upside to Parkinson's it's that it's brought out a strength in us that was always there but has now been hardened and sharpened on the anvil of adversity. We don't know what we're made of until, like a precious metal, we've been through the refiner's fire and the dross is removed."

"Wow, I'm impressed with the poet in you." I laugh.

He drops his arm and I reach for his hand. The sun begins to drop beyond the horizon leaving golden to red hues in its wake. We stop and watch the sunset develop until the light retracts and the heavens become a darkening void.

I break the silence. "I can't help but wonder what it would have been like to suffer Parkinson's before it was understood and before any drugs. Take my poor ancestor Mary. Life must have been tough back then for Parkinson's sufferers."

"I imagine being misunderstood would have forced them to hide from the world."

"Don't get me wrong, having Parkinson's today is no easy road. For some, the symptoms are unbearably bad, especially those relating to psychiatric disorders." I squeeze his hand. "But thank goodness for modern medicine and for all the researchers beavering away to make our lives better."

"I've no doubt we are blessed to be living in this place and in this time."

"I'm very thankful for that. It could easily have been so different." I turn to this man who has promised to love me through sickness and health. "Given we are so blessed to have this life I don't want to waste a single day. For as long as I live I don't ever want to lose sight of hope. Hope for a cure, hope for our future, eternal hope. I choose to put my faith in hope."

"Amen to that."

Author's Note

The story of Mary Black is one of pure fiction, as is the character Elizabeth. I have included Mary's story to remind us of how far we have come in the last two hundred years. I like to think I am incredibly blessed to live in this place and at this time in history. So much more is understood about Parkinson's disease today and there is still more to be discovered. I believe we are on the brink of solving the condition that is called Parkinson's disease and a cure will be found in my lifetime.

On the other hand, James Parkinson (1755–1824) did live and practise as a physician in Hoxton in the early nineteenth century. He is credited with publishing *An Essay on the Shaking Palsy* in 1817 which set out a closely-observed, clinical account of a progressive, disabling condition affecting the nervous system. His essay described the condition in three of his own patients and three persons whom he saw in the street. The condition was renamed as *Parkinson's Disease* in 1865. In addition to his work as a physician James Parkinson was a political activist and writer of political pamphlets, a pioneer in the reformation of public health and an advocate for infection control in London workhouses, a medical attendant to a Hoxton madhouse, a geologist and palaeontologist, and the author of a textbook on chemistry.

Perhaps James Parkinson's character is best described by his own words written in a pamphlet: *[A] sympathetic concern, and a tender interest for the sufferings of others [that] ought to characterise all those who engage themselves in a profession, the object of which should be to mitigate, or remove, one great portion of the calamities to which humanity is subject.*

Mary and Me

Did You Know?

Some Interesting Facts About Parkinson's Disease[1]

1. Parkinson's disease is the fastest-growing neurological condition in the world.
2. Parkinson's disease affects more than ten million people worldwide.
3. Approximately 1 in 100 people over the age of 60 have Parkinson's disease.
4. The average age at diagnosis is 59 years.
5. One in 20 people with Parkinson's disease first develop symptoms under the age of 40.
6. Men are 1.5 times more likely to have Parkinson's disease than women.
7. Constipation and a loss of smell can be early symptoms and one theory is that Parkinson's starts in the gut or in the area of the brain responsible for the sense of smell.
8. Parkinson's is caused by the degeneration and loss of nerve cells that produce a substance called dopamine deep in the brain. The main area affected is known as the substantia nigra. Dopamine is an important chemical messenger involved in the regulation of movement. Loss of dopamine results in the characteristic symptoms of slowed movement and tremor.

9. Parkinson's is not just a movement disorder. People with Parkinson's can have other symptoms such as changes in mood and cognition, low blood pressure and disturbed sleep.
10. The cause of Parkinson's is unknown. Research has focused on potential environmental triggers, including exposure to chemicals used in pesticides and herbicides, heavy metals and head injuries.
11. There is currently no known cure, but there are treatments that can help manage symptoms.
12. Exercise helps maintain mobility and there are indications it may change the trajectory of the disease.
13. Fewer than 10% of people diagnosed with Parkinson's have a genetic link to the condition.
14. There are numerous research projects worldwide, either searching for a cure or a means to slow the progression of the disease or targeting interventions to better manage the symptoms.

[1] This list has been approved by the Medical Advisory Panel at Parkinson's New Zealand

Glossary

Apathy Lack of interest, enthusiasm, or concern.

Autonomic nervous system Automatically regulates certain body processes such as blood pressure, respiratory system, digestion, urination...

Bradykinesia Impaired and slow movement of limbs of the body.

Dopamine A compound present in the body as a neurotransmitter and a precursor of other substances, including epinephrine.

Dyskinesia Abnormality or impairment of voluntary movement.

Dystonia A movement disorder in which your muscles contract involuntarily, causing repetitive or twisting movements.

Essential tremor A benign nervous system disorder that causes rhythmic shaking.

Keto diet	An extremely low carbohydrate diet that aims to promote the metabolism of fats into ketone bodies (rather than carbohydrates into glucose) to provide the body's main source of energy.
Ketosis	A metabolic state characterised by raised levels of ketone bodies in the body tissues.
Levodopa	A drug used to treat Parkinson's disease.
Lewy bodies	Abnormal aggregates of protein that develop inside nerve cells.
Neuroplasticity	The ability of the brain to form and reorganise synaptic connections, especially in response to a learning experience or following injury.
Olfactory	Relating to the sense of smell.
Palsy	Paralysis, especially when accompanied by involuntary tremors.
Substantia nigra	A basal ganglia structure located in the midbrain that plays an important role in reward and movement.

A SKYLARK FLIES

Robyn Cotton

Rose, a young Kiwi, is on a working holiday in the United Kingdom, to discover her roots. When in Scotland she is subjected to a brutal assault by a local man, Tommy.

Their lives will never be the same again. While Rose fights to recover from her emotional trauma Tommy, a victim of a lifetime of abuse, struggles with guilt. The choices they make will ultimately determine whether they live life as victims or rise above it.

Inspired by true events A Skylark Flies is a poignant story of forgiveness. It gives the reader a window into the souls of two very different characters whose stories converge at critical points.

The assailant has power over the victim, induced by fear—and the victim has power to release him from his guilt and shame.

Available from DayStar Books (info@daystarbooks.org) or the author (rmcotton.hatherop@gmail.com)

Robyn Cotton grew up in South Taranaki and studied at Massey University in Palmerston North, before embarking on a career in the dairy industry and as a management consultant. In recent years she has put her energy into governance. Her creative writing is inspired by her own experience and has led to *Mary and Me*, her second novel. Robyn is a Christian living with Parkinson's disease and enjoys time with her family, photography, travel, sailing and exploring New Zealand's unique natural environment.